Finding Walter

Ann Turner

Finding Walter

HARCOURT BRACE & COMPANY

San Diego   New York   London

Library of Congress Cataloging-in-Publication Data
Turner, Ann Warren.
Finding Walter/Ann Turner.
p.   cm.
Summary: When she, her sister Rose, and her parents come to live in her
grandmother's old country house, eight-year-old Emily draws them
all into her efforts to find the youngest of a neglected family of dolls.
ISBN 0-15-200212-X
[1. Dolls—Fiction.   2. Family life—Fiction.   3. Sisters—
Fiction.   4. Moving, Household—Fiction.]   I. Title.
PZ7.T8535Fi   1997
[Fic]—dc20   96-4197

First edition   A B C D E F
Text set in Fairfield
Designed by Camilla Filancia

Printed in the United States of America

J Fil

To my daughter, Charlotte

Finding Walter

chapter 1

THE TROUBLE was the mice. And the moths. Sometimes the spiders. They had taken over the dollhouse that lay in the attic, out of sight, forgotten since Alice had grown up and gone away. The moths lived in the top floor of the dollhouse, a high room with a steeply pitched roof. There were two beds snugged under the eaves, dolls tucked under the tattered covers. The blankets had once been a bright red and blue, clear as fall leaves against a crisp sky. Now they were faded to an ugly gray with moth holes in them.

The trouble with the moths is that they liked to lie

about. They rested on the beds and hung their wings out to dry. The dollhouse was a perfect place for them when they were just moving from their cocoons into the real world, rather like a hospital for a newborn baby. The dolls said nothing, knowing their words no longer made any difference. Sad things happen to dolls when they are not played with and are left to languish in a dark attic for twenty years.

Then there were the mice. Hundreds of them had come and gone since Alice last played with the dolls. They were mice just like any other mice—opportunists, looking for the main chance. They scampered down the drainpipes at night and seized crumbs from the pantry, bringing them upstairs to the attic to chew and dream over. They scampered up and down the steep dollhouse stairs, staging races and laps. The older mice curled up on the beds and had long, dreamless sleeps. And, of course, they left their droppings everywhere, like little black seeds that would never grow into anything.

Then there were the spiders, a brown race of creatures who liked the pool of darkness at the foot of the stairs. They made webs in the corners of the living room and the dining room. It was a fine Victorian dining room, with a long table draped in white cloth and pewter dishes ranged along the side. Tiny forks and knives lay beside the places, and small, delicate glass tumblers held a faint purple smear from the grape juice Alice had poured for the feast on that last day the dolls had lived.

That is what Emily saw the day she found the dollhouse. It had a fusty, musty smell and looked rather frightening with all the bits and pieces left out, as if someone had meant to come back to play but had suddenly been seized by cholera and died before their time.

"Look!" Emily tugged on Rose's arm. "It's a dollhouse. Papa said it was here, that his sister Alice used to play with it."

Rose came and knelt before it, brushing the bits of cotton wool away from the floor. "But it's filthy, Emily. Look at the upstairs." She pointed to the faded spreads and the mice droppings that speckled the floors and furniture. "Phew! It stinks!"

"Well, so would you if you had been left to all these mice and..." Emily waved her hand, unsure of what or who else lived in the dollhouse. She touched the staircase and then snatched her hand away. Her fingers were black and sticky with bits of spiderweb. "Ugh!" she exclaimed, wiping her hand on her shorts.

"See? Filthy!" Rose said her favorite word. "Simply filthy. You'd do better to have a nice modern dollhouse with clean floors and..."

"No thank you." Emily carefully picked up one of the dolls from the attic bedroom. "Look, her head, feet, and hands are china." She touched the girl doll in a torn dress. "And the rest is wood." Emily spit on her handkerchief and wiped the doll's face. Two blue eyes peered up at her, and roses bloomed on her cheeks.

She held up the doll. "See how bright her face is?"

In spite of herself, Rose was interested. "I wonder what her name is."

The doll whispered, "Violet is my name. Violet, like

the flower, you know, soft and purple and coming out in the spring. I know all about love and flowers."

But Rose and Emily did not hear, for her words were spoken in a tone too far away from that of human speech.

Holding her breath, so as not to breathe in all the dust, Rose picked up a boy doll dressed in faded blue pants and a sailor shirt. His straw hat was long gone, taken by the mice for their nests. Rose spit on her handkerchief and wiped the boy's face, uncovering two green eyes and red cheeks. A grin was painted on his face, and brown hair stuck out above his ears.

"Oh, doesn't he look naughty!" said Rose. "Doesn't he look like he put toads in that girl doll's bed..."

"I did," whispered the boy.

"...and threw spiders at her. His name should be Billy or something," Rose finished, laughing.

"Billy it is," said Emily.

"Actually, my full name is William," said the boy doll, "but if you insist, I will accept Billy."

"Who else is there?" Rose searched through the house, roughly pulling out pieces of furniture and dusty rugs.

"Careful, there's a lot of bugs and moths in there. They might stir up your allergies, Rose."

Her sister sneezed, as predicted, and blew her nose on the not-very-clean handkerchief with which she'd wiped Billy's face. "We'll have to get some things to clean the house—a bowl of soapy water and some brushes and paper towels."

"Oh good, I was afraid you weren't going to like it,"

Emily said, almost dancing as she looked at the house. "This will give us something to do before school starts next month." She stopped as Rose glared at her.

"I still don't see why we had to move, but Daddy believed whatever that doctor said," Rose grumbled.

"Well, so did Mother. She was afraid, remember?" And so were we, Emily wanted to add—tiptoeing around the house while Daddy was ill, the air dark and heavy the way it is before a thunderstorm and full of a strange, sharp smell. And so they had come to live with Gran in her house for a year while Daddy's heart got better, away from the city, away from his job.

"Mmmmm," mumbled Rose.

"Still," said Emily. "This is ours. Daddy said it could be. And once it's clean, it will be perfect!"

Emily's words hung over the dollhouse like little bright balloons. The dolls shivered inside, excited and afraid.

"Where are Mama and Papa?" asked Violet, wishing she could get up and run about the house, looking. She would throw her stiff arms around Mama, for she had not seen her in ages. All this time they had slept the deep sleep of dolls who are not played with. Occasionally Violet had stirred slightly, hearing a sound. She never knew if it was mice or something else. Sometimes she would wake and see moonlight slanting in through the window across their floor. And she would think, *Someday we will be alive again. Someday we will sing songs at night, and a girl will pick me up and play with me.*

She remembered the places Alice had taken her long

ago: to the butternut tree outside, down to the garden where pink peonies bloomed so huge and sweet-smelling that Violet never knew if she really saw them or only dreamed them.

"This little girl," Violet said, looking at the one with the sticking-out braids and her tongue caught between her teeth. "This is the one. She will love me and I will love her, and I will forget that long time under the covers with mice and spiders running over me."

"Where are Mama and Papa?" William called. "I can't hear them, can you?"

"We are here; we are here!" Papa's voice rose faintly. "We're just waiting for them to collect and clean us. Oh, dear ones! I see happiness like golden balloons over our house."

"We can't wait to see you!" Mama cried out. "William? Violet? Walter?"

"Here," cried William.

"Here," answered Violet.

But only silence echoed after the call for Walter.

chapter 2

"Phew! What is that?" Mama doll sneezed as Rose sprayed a blast of cleanser into a second-story bedroom.

"Wait, wait!" Emily said. "Let's get everybody out before we start cleaning."

Together the girls dragged the dollhouse into the middle of the attic, where sunlight from a high window shone down on the floorboards. Rose sneezed.

"Dust! Can't be good for my allergies."

"Nothing's good for your allergies," Emily said. "Come on. Let's see who else lives here."

From the second floor she drew out a bed with a

tattered spread. On it lay a lady doll who had black hair in a wispy bun, a torn blue dress, and tiny black slippers.

"Look, Rose, the mice didn't get her shoes."

"Though it wasn't for want of trying," whispered Mama doll.

"I wonder what her name is?" Emily dusted the lady doll and wiped her face with a clean cloth.

"Hettie," said Mama doll, "short for Henrietta, of course, though my father never called me that. It was always 'Hettie' this and 'Hettie' that, until I grew to love it. Mind you, I didn't like my name at first. It takes me a long time to like things."

Emily stared at the painted cornflower blue eyes. "This doll has personality," she said. "She likes to lie in bed at night and make up stories."

"How do you know that?" whispered Hettie. "Are you magic as well as big? Violet, is that you?" she called down to her daughter, who was lying in front of the dollhouse on a rug.

"Yes, Mama, it's me, at last! Welcome to the world."

"And William, is that you? Oh, how I've missed you both!"

"Yes, Mama, I'm here, too, and we will all be together again," called William from his place beside Violet.

"Look," Rose said, taking a doll out from the downstairs parlor. "He must be the papa doll." He was tall and thin with black hair and wrists that hung out from his frayed cuffs. His bowtie had come undone and hung limply on his gray shirtfront. He looked as if he were dressed for a Victorian evening at home, in black pants and a smoking jacket.

Rose dusted his clothes, sneezed again, and wiped his face and hands. "I wonder what his name is? Just Papa doll?"

"Arthur," he said slowly, "like the king of England, like a brave knight, don't you know? I am lionhearted, although no one knows that because I've only lived in this house or sometimes outside under the butternut tree. I wish I could have adventures. Hello, Hettie, Violet, and William! Walter must still be sleeping, eh?"

Hettie cried out when she saw him in Rose's hand. "Arthur! Whatever happened to your tie? You never used to be so sloppy. And your poor suit! What happened to your pipe and your paper? Oh, Arthur, I've missed you so."

"There, there, Hettie, everything will be all right. These two girls will fix us up in no time and get the house clean. Then we can live the way we used to."

"Used to," sighed Hettie, William, and Violet.

"They must be a family," Rose said, busily arranging them on a box cover nearby. "The papa doll, the mama doll, the girl doll, and the boy."

"Where's Walter?" whispered Hettie. "Where's my little boy?"

"Someone should wake up Walter!" cried Papa.

"We haven't seen him since that Last Day We Lived," chimed Violet and William together.

Emily took out each piece of furniture one by one

and sprayed it. "Dining-room table," she said, taking off the soiled cloth and all the tiny utensils and plates. "Doesn't it look scary, Rose? All these things left out and the dried purple something in the glasses?" She held one up to the light.

"Everything scares you," snapped Rose, irritated by the black dust that caught in her nose.

"It does not!" Emily sat back on her heels. Her chest hurt, as if Rose's words had flashed across, scorching her skin. But she would not cry—not in front of Rose.

Violet looked sympathetically at her. "Poor thing. You can see she's just bullied by that great red-faced..."

"Hush!" William said. "We think they can't hear, but sometimes if everything works just right, they *do* understand."

Violet stopped talking and thought her words instead.

Emily finished cleaning the dining-room furniture and packed the things away in a shoebox lined with tissue paper so nothing should be broken. Then she began on the kitchen. It was a wide, deep room with darkness caught in the far corners. Emily worked at the corners with her wet cloth and wiped up clumps of dirt, dead moths, and dried spiders.

"Ugh!" Shuddering, she threw the cloth away, taking up a fresh one. Now that the grime was gone, she saw that the floor of the kitchen was a pretty blue-and-white tile. A Welsh dresser filled with little blue-and-white plates and cups stood against the near wall.

"Willow ware," said Rose, thrusting her face into the

kitchen. "Mother'll love to see all those tiny cups and saucers."

"Will she?" Emily said faintly. She wasn't sure if she wanted Mother looking at this dollhouse. She might try to take it in hand and decorate it, and then it wouldn't be their special project anymore.

Rose was at work on the second-floor bedrooms. She'd taken out three beds with badly torn spreads, three dressers of a lovely soft brown, and some rugs that were more holes than cloth.

"We'll have to get a lot of new things for it," Rose said, almost angrily. "How will we pay for it? Out of our allowance?"

"Maybe," Emily said. There was always Grandmother. She knew about things like dollhouses having to be just so and old furniture needing to be fixed up and loved. Maybe Gran would make some rugs for them and curtains if they asked.

"Where is Walter?" Hettie asked again. "When did you last see him, Violet?"

"We were in the far right-hand bedroom that Last Day when Alice played with us," Violet mused. "Weren't we, William?"

"Mmmm." He was watching all this activity with great interest, amazed at the energy of the two girls. He thought he liked the one with the sticking-out, not-quite-blond pigtails best. She caught her tongue between her teeth when she was wiping the kitchen floor. And she had nice ears, neat and close to her head under the tight plaits.

Once William had seen a page from an old-fashioned book that said ears like hers were a sign of good character.

The other one was big and pink, with a little dent in her chin. William believed that meant you had a cruel disposition. Then he remembered he was supposed to be answering Violet's question.

"Yes, we were in the right-hand bedroom on the Last Day when Alice played with us. Walter was drinking milk from a cup. I remember he spilled it down the front of his shirt, and Alice just left him there, all covered with milk. Maybe the squirrels in the attic..." When Violet flashed him a look of warning, he suddenly stopped.

But Hettie heard, and she gasped. "Maybe Walter is somewhere else in the big house. You remember that loud boy, Alice's older brother?"

Papa nodded and cleared his throat. "He never liked us very much."

Hettie went on, "He could have taken Walter, just to annoy Alice."

"Maybe," Papa sighed, missing Walter so much that his heart ached.

It took all afternoon, but finally everything was clean. Emily and Rose had sprayed and wiped down every single room in the house: the downstairs parlor, the kitchen, the dining room, the three upstairs bedrooms, and the high, wide attic. They'd even washed the stairs, wiping each tread with a wadded-up cloth. Having scrubbed the outside of the house, too, the girls were now thoroughly filthy.

"Mother will not be pleased." Rose dusted off her dress.

"No," agreed Emily, "she won't. But Daddy will like it that we found the dollhouse and got it all fixed up. Remember he sometimes talked about it and how Alice would play with it for hours?"

"Mmmmm." Rose swabbed her face with a wet cloth.

"What do we do now?" Emily asked.

"I'm too tired to put the furniture back," Rose said, and sighed. "I still don't have my room fixed up yet."

"Let's put the dolls in their beds," suggested Emily. "They'll need somewhere to live until we arrange everything."

Carefully the girls placed all four dolls on the clean, bare beds in front of the dollhouse and spread squares of Kleenex over them.

"Do you think we're going to like it here?" Emily asked suddenly.

"Probably not! We'll have to make all new friends; it's in the country, not a museum in sight, not a park..." Rose's voice trailed off.

"But it's better for Daddy's heart, that's what the doctor said."

"I don't see why the country is better for bad hearts than the city!" Rose snapped. "Did you hear the noise this morning outside our windows? PEEP, PEEP, PEEP. Those birds are very noisy!"

Emily made a murmuring sound but did not answer. She'd learned that when Rose was mad, it was sometimes better not to talk. She stood, looking at the dollhouse for the last time that day. Now she could go to bed in her new bedroom thinking of the cleaned dollhouse, with all the dolls and their furniture lined up, ready to be played with.

As the girls disappeared down the attic stairs, Hettie said again, in a worried voice, "But where is Walter? Did the girls find him?"

"No," said Papa, fumbling in his pocket where his pipe used to be. "No, but he's bound to be here somewhere." The words sounded empty in the dark, echoing space of the attic.

Violet shook her head and said nothing. In the dim half-sleep they had inhabited for twenty years, waiting for someone to love them to life again, she remembered the faint cries the other dolls had made as they dreamed. She had never heard Walter's voice, not once.

chapter 3

EMILY DREAMED of the dollhouse. There was a twittering and squeaking sound, like mice, and in the dream someone tried to run upstairs. The mother doll waved a tattered handkerchief and shrieked, "We've lost Walter! My boy's gone. Who took him, who?" She swayed, clutched the banister, and suddenly fell with a clattering of tiny feet.

"Oh, Hettie! Are you all right, dear?" cried Papa doll. He started toward her with jerky little steps.

"Yes," sighed Mama doll. "I'm all right. It's these

dratted feet of mine! We've lain for so long without moving that my limbs are like wood!"

"Perhaps that's because they *are* wood, Hettie, dear." Papa smiled. "But we just don't know where Walter is. We know he was in the right-hand bedroom the last time we saw him, when Alice spilled milk on him, and we know when the girls woke us up yesterday, Walter was gone. He's not necessarily *taken*."

"Gone," sighed the golden-haired girl doll, "gone. No one to love anymore. I can't live if I can't love; you know that. I must have flowers, and I must have Walter back to hold on my lap and sing to." She pressed her hand dramatically to her brow.

The boy doll snapped, "Stop it, Violet! Hasn't Mama enough to do without you carrying on? We all want Walter back."

Violet gave him a tragic look and sighed. "You don't understand about love, William. I think you have no heart."

"Of course I do!" declared William. But he wasn't exactly sure just what a heart was and if he had one.

"Who would take a little boy doll?" Hettie asked, slowly pulling herself upright by the banister. "Do you think that Alice's brother, the one with the puffy nose, took him somewhere?"

Papa said, "I don't know, dear heart; we'll just have to keep looking. Maybe he's in another part of the big attic. And you forget—we can call to Walter. If he's awake, he will hear us and send us a message."

"But what if he's not awake?" Violet asked sharply.

"We were asleep until those girls found us and picked us up. What if he's lost somewhere?"

"Violet!" Papa scolded, looking at Hettie. "We will find him; don't worry." But his voice quavered and ended on a rising note.

Emily woke and sat bolt upright in bed. The sorrow of the dolls wrapped around her throat like a tight collar. She pulled at her nightgown and took in deep breaths of the sweet morning air.

"What's wrong with you?" Rose asked. She had slept in Emily's room last night, saying that her room was full of "thumps and squeaks" and she wouldn't, couldn't, sleep there all by herself.

Emily stared out the window. "They've lost their little brother," she whispered. "I dreamed it, except it didn't seem like a dream at all. He was there on the Last Day when Alice played with them—I guess something happens to dolls when no one plays with them; I'm not exactly sure what—and Alice spilled milk all down his front. I think they're afraid something or somebody took Walter."

"Who's Walter?" mumbled Rose, scratching her nose and sneezing three times in a row.

"The little boy, the one they've lost, and Violet says she has to have Walter back to sing to."

"Little boy? Violet?" Rose sat up in bed and peered at her sister. "Who *are* these people, Emily? You're not making sense!"

Emily put her bare feet on the floorboards. "The youngest doll is named Walter, and he is lost. That's what

I've been telling you! And Violet," she said, peeling off her nightgown and pulling on khaki shorts and a red T-shirt, "is the girl doll we found yesterday in the doll-house. She knows all about love and flowers."

"How do you know that?" Rose came and stood in front of her sister.

"She told me," Emily said impatiently, tying her sneakers.

"Oh, Emily, that's just a dream! Dolls can't talk; they don't have feelings." Rose rubbed her nose frantically, trying to get at an inside itch.

Emily tried to push past her. "Maybe they *can* talk, but we can't hear them. And maybe they *do* have feelings but just can't tell them. Now, will you get out of my way, Rose? I'm going to have breakfast and look for Walter."

Stepping aside, Rose watched her sister leave the room, and her chest felt hot. Her head was itchy and uncomfortable, and she wanted to hit someone.

Gran sat at the head of the table, her hair a silver cloud around her face. She watched as Emily got herself a bowl, spoon, cereal, and milk.

"Sleep well, child?"

"Oh, yes, Gran." Emily sat at the table. "Except for this strange dream I had about the dolls upstairs in the dollhouse, the one that Alice left with nothing put away. She never cleaned up Walter, who had milk all down his shirt. Isn't that appalling?" *Appalling* was Emily's favorite word this month.

Gran sipped her tea, cradling the cup in her thin

hands. "It is appalling. Alice always was a careless child. Who's Walter?"

"The little boy in the doll family. They can't find him, or rather, we can't find him. When we cleaned the doll-house yesterday we found Papa doll, Hettie—she's the mother—Violet and Billy, though William is his real name." Emily paused and had two large spoonfuls of granola. "Anyway, Walter's lost and I think they're afraid something or somebody got him."

Gran bit into a piece of toast with butter spread out to the very edges, the way she liked it. "Do they think Alice went off with Walter?"

"They don't know what to think, Gran. But I'm going to help them," she said happily, taking her bowl to the sink.

"Hi, sweetie!" Dad came into the kitchen, patted Emily's head, and sat expectantly at the table. "Did the birds wake you up?" He didn't wait for an answer; he never did. "They woke me up at five o'clock—worse than traffic."

Gran said mildly, "There's a bran muffin in the toaster oven, Henry, and coffee on the counter."

"Bran?" he said unhappily, rising and poking at the object in the toaster.

"Of course." Mother came in and poured herself some coffee. "Remember what the doctor said?"

"I remember him saying I can't eat any of the things worth eating, Marge." Gingerly he slid the muffin onto a plate, sat down, and stared at it.

Emily escaped out of the kitchen. She did not want to hear her parents talking about sickness or getting well. It made her feel shivery, like fingernails scraping down a blackboard. She was going looking for Walter.

She ran up the stairs two at a time to the attic. She gathered the dolls in her hands, took them downstairs, and through the front door to the butternut tree. She guessed Rose was eating breakfast; she hadn't seen her.

"There." Emily settled the dolls with their backs against the butternut tree. "Maybe you can find Walter out here or call to him." She sat on a swing nearby.

"We *think* to him, dear," Hettie said in her quiet voice. "He hears us thinking."

"Though a few good yells never hurt anybody," said Papa doll. "Ah, this child knows how to live. I haven't had fresh air in years." He peered up through the leaves to the sky—he guessed it was the sky, those great blobs of blue sliding and splashing about along with the green. It had been such a long time, he'd almost forgotten.

Violet slipped down against the base of the tree to lie on her back. She had long ago learned how to manage motion so that it looked like an accident. Sunlight drenched her face and she smiled. "Oh, what a lovely, lovely girl we've got ourselves this time."

"We don't *get* girls," chided William, "and don't forget, there's another girl here, too, the one with the dent in her chin. I think she is an angry one, and we will have to be careful of her."

"Fuss, fuss, William," said Violet, humming softly to

herself. "What else can we want? Sunlight, air, and bird-song." Then she stopped humming and sighed. "Walter, that's what else we need. I forgot for a moment. Aren't we going to call to him?"

"Thank you for reminding us, sweet Violet," said Papa. In a commanding tone of voice he announced, "On the count of three, call to Walter. Say: Walter, where are you? We love you and want you home. Where are you? One, two, three!"

Their words spun out in all directions—some to the woods, some over the meadow, some back to the house. They waited and waited, but there was no response.

"Maybe he is still asleep," Hettie said in a trying-to-be-brave voice.

"That's right, dear. We mustn't give up hope," said Papa.

From the swing Emily glanced down at the dolls. They looked worn and a little sad. Maybe Walter hadn't answered their calls. Then what? She heard the screen door slam, and Rose ran across the grass.

"Who is it?" Violet was suddenly frightened. A gigantic face peered down at her, then a hot hand seized her and held her tightly.

"Is this Violet?" Rose asked Emily.

Nervously Emily got off the swing and came nearer. "That's Violet. Don't hold her so tightly, Rose. She doesn't like it."

"Like it? How come you know so much about dolls, Em?" The hot feeling inside Rose expanded. She felt as if her chest needed a good scratch, but that wasn't it. Something black and crinkly was at the back of her mind, worrying Rose until the words shot out of her.

"We'll see how she likes *this,* Em!" And she tossed Violet high up in the butternut tree, where the doll caught in some tangled leaves.

Emily pushed her. "So big, so bossy—why couldn't you leave her alone! Now look!"

Rose didn't shove back; she just smiled. "Now Violet can learn all about love. She can watch the birds." She walked back to the house, banging the screen door behind her.

Emily sighed. "Don't worry, Violet," she called up through the leaves. "I'll get you down somehow." She went off to the garden shed. Violet was quite high up, and only a ladder would do, she decided.

"Are you all right, dear?" called Hettie from down below in the grass.

Violet lay stiff and frightened in a nest of withered leaves. Anything could happen! A weasel could carry her off, or an eagle. Woodpeckers—didn't they like to peck at old wood? Shivering, Violet watched a bird settle on the branch overhead. It jumped down to investigate, cocking its head and staring at her with bright, inquisitive eyes. Violet yelled at the bird and it flew away. Then a fly came and landed on her nose.

She sneezed. "This is not the way it should be. Not at all."

Emily came out from the back shed, dragging a step-ladder. She leaned it against the butternut tree and climbed as high as she dared. Holding out her arm, she tried to shake Violet loose, but she was too far away.

"Oh, Violet. Don't give up hope. I'll try and get a taller ladder." She clambered down and went inside, banging the screen door.

"Don't give up hope, Violet." Papa repeated Emily's words. "She'll come back; I'm sure of it."

"Yes," nodded William. "She has a good character; you can tell from her ears."

Finally the screen door slammed again, and Emily ran out to them, scooping up the dolls in her warm hands. "I'm sorry, dolls, but I've been trying to get a ladder for Violet. We'll have to wait till our neighbor comes home from work. I'll be back, Violet, around suppertime."

Violet cried out as her family was carried away. She heard the faint voice of her mother calling, "Good-bye, Violet; don't be afraid." As Violet stared upward, the sun swung across the sky. She thought sharp, hurtful thoughts about that big girl with the pink face. It was all *her* fault.

Inside the house Rose gasped and clutched her chest suddenly, as she sat and did a puzzle at the table.

chapter 4

WALTER LAY on a heap of leaves. His painted nose and mouth had slipped sideways, dragged there by years of dripping water and ice. His joints were coming unglued, and when he moved, his left arm wobbled. Sometimes when the stars were bright and moonlight flooded the woods, he woke and stirred a little. Vaguely he remembered a house he'd once lived in. Another doll with soft, golden hair had loved him and held him on her lap.

He moaned softly when he remembered that. And

two big dolls had carried him about and murmured sweet things to him. Someone big had once given him milk. It got him into trouble. Another *very* big and angry person had taken him off that same afternoon and left him outside in the grass. Then Big Nose came and sniffed him all over. It nibbled his shirt off, and a wet, hot tongue lapped him again and again, until he was dripping wet. Then sharp, white teeth picked him up and carried him to this dark hole in the earth. A little more nibbling, and the teeth suddenly dropped him. Giving a short, sharp bark, Big Nose disappeared.

Walter fell into the earth that was sometimes warm and sometimes bitterly cold. Mice chewed the rest of his clothes off until he was naked. Crawling things with hundreds of legs scurried over him. Once a great bird peered at him, its golden eye shining into the burrow. Then it flapped away.

But now, in the abandoned fox's den, Walter stirred. Something dove into his hole in the earth and a faraway voice called in his ear.

Walter, where are you? We love you and want you home. Where are you?

Walter turned over and sighed. What was love? What was home? It was all too much trouble. Sleeping was so much better.

Violet wished she could close her eyes and shut out the sunlight. The sky was so *busy*! Birds here, birds there, talking and calling. Didn't they know how to be quiet?

Then she shivered. What if a raccoon climbed up the tree to carry her off? What if a crow lurched out of the sky to take her to some filthy nest?

"Nonsense!" Violet said stoutly. "They want live things to eat—not me!" That made her feel better, and she tried to imagine what her family would be doing inside the dollhouse. If that nice girl had put them in the parlor, William would be sitting on the flowered sofa. Papa might be beside him, with a worried frown on his face. Mama could be standing by the plastic fern, trying to be brave and hopeful.

The great ball sank in the sky, the air turned purple, and finally black. Where was the girl? Where was rescue? To keep up her spirits, Violet began to sing to herself, in a high, wavery voice, songs Mama had sung to her when she was new. One had the word *hush-a-bye* in it, and the sound comforted Violet. Everything will be all right; you'll see, Violet told herself. "Good things happen to the good"—wasn't that what William said? And she was definitely good. Soon that nice girl would come back with a long ladder. Soon she would be rescued and be with her family once again.

She sighed happily when she heard footsteps below.

"Violet?" the girl called up. "I'm awfully sorry, but I can't get you down tonight. Mr. White, the next-door neighbor, isn't home yet, and we're supposed to get the ladder from him. Please don't be afraid. Nothing can harm you up there, and I'll be back in the morning."

Violet would have cried if she could. Instead she listened to the girl's footsteps receding across the lawn, to the house. The door closing was such a final sound that she gasped. Alone—in a tree—at night. Is Walter out here, too? Again she thought to him, sending out messages, but there were no answering words. Sad and frightened, Violet finally pulled a leaf over her head to block out the night and slept.

chapter 5

VIOLET WATCHED dawn come to the sky: first a tinge of pink; yellow crept in; then the great golden ball rose in the sky. It blazed through the leaves and shone full in her face. A blue jay jumped on the branch above, crying out. He startled the resting cicadas; their thick bodies bustled with indignation. One of them dropped on Violet's stomach and scurried off before she could shriek. The blue jay continued to shake his wings and scream at the world.

Later on, when the crows flew up into the pale sky,

Violet heard the house door slamming. A car drove in and scrunched on gravel. Below came a man's voice and the sound of metal against tree bark. *At last, a ladder!* Violet thought. She heard steps climbing up and saw a head appearing through the leaves. It was the nice girl, with a worried frown on her face.

"Oh, I hope you're all right, Violet. Were you frightened?" She reached out a warm, grubby hand and lifted the doll gently by her waist.

"Here, we'll be down in a minute. Close your eyes if you want to." Emily backed down the ladder and stood on the grass again. "There! Now we're set."

"All right now?" said a large man with a weathered face, dark hair, and green suspenders.

"Yes, thanks." Emily smiled at him. "She's a little wet from the dew, but that won't hurt her."

Violet watched the wrinkles crease around the man's mouth as he laughed loudly. "A little dew never hurt anyone! Well, I'll be taking my ladder back now. If you need any help, remember, I'm right next door. White's my name; helping is my game." He saluted to Emily and Violet, turned, climbed into his battered truck, and drove off.

"What a nice man," Emily said. "Now everyone else is back in the dollhouse. I'm sure they've been wondering how you are. I'll take you there right now."

She ran inside, past Rose, who was struggling with a complicated puzzle. Emily shot out as she went by, "If Violet gets pneumonia, it'll be your fault! All night in the butternut tree just because you had to toss her up and show how smart you are!"

Before Rose could frame a satisfactory reply, something that would have included, "Dolls don't get sick; you're making it all up," her sister was gone.

Emily raced up to the attic and set Violet on her bed in the upstairs room. She patted her face dry with a soft, pink coverlet.

"Oh, this is nice; when did you put this on my bed?" Violet asked.

"Violet, is that you?" Hettie called from downstairs. Emily had put her in the kitchen, making a batch of muffins for breakfast.

"Yes, Mama, I'm back, after *quite* a time! I never knew it was so noisy outside. 'Chirp, chirp, chirp,' went the crickets all night long. It's a wonder I got any sleep at all."

"Poor thing," Mama said. "You'd better have a little rest."

Emily patted Violet's face again and tucked her under the cover. "Have a nap, Violet, and you'll feel much better. Your mother is making muffins downstairs, the nice kind with nuts and bits of raisins. I snipped them myself."

Looking proudly into the kitchen, Emily grinned at the small containers filled with flour, sugar, bits of raisins, and slivers of nuts. But she missed the look of confusion on Hettie's face.

Violet sighed happily. "Aren't we lucky to have this girl? William, where are you?"

William replied from the parlor, "Yes, we are lucky to have her, but don't forget the other one with the pink face. She's the one who threw you into the butternut, and she will do worse before her time is out, mark my words."

William liked to make pronouncements in a round, full voice. Once he'd been taken to church in Alice's pocket, and he had fallen in love with the preacher's voice—rich and plummy, with a purple sound to it. At times William could be heard murmuring, "Woe unto you, oh ye hypocrites," though he had no idea what it meant. But the words felt so full and satisfying in his mouth, he just had to say them.

"William, time to come to breakfast." Emily sat him at the table.

Hettie said in a bustling voice, "Do you want tea with your muffins, William?"

He saw steam rising gently from a small china pot with blue flowers on it. "Oh, my, how the righteous are rewarded!" he crowed.

"Don't talk like that, William," snapped Hettie. There was sweat on her brow, she was sure of it, for she'd never made muffins before. Or anything else, for that matter. Alice hadn't taught her, and she was struggling to remember what her own mother had put into the mix.

"Baking soda," she murmured, "sugar, I think..."

Emily reached in and gave the flour in the bowl a big stir. "That's it, Hettie; you've got it now!"

"But we don't have any eggs!" Hettie exclaimed. "Mother said muffins must have eggs."

Emily could see a faint, worried pucker between Hettie's eyebrows, but she didn't know what caused it or, indeed, if she always looked this way. She touched the doll's shoulder briefly and said, "I'll pour the tea—you cook." Emily filled three small cups and set them on the table. Sitting Papa at the head of the table, she tucked a small white bib around his throat. The fourth cup she left by Violet's bed.

"My," breathed Violet, who was wide awake. "Tea in bed! Alice never did that."

"Alice never did anything," Papa said from the kitchen, "except spill food on our shirts and get Walter lost."

Suddenly the dolls' chatter stopped and gloom descended on the house. "I forgot," William whispered. "I was so excited to have real tea at last."

"So was I," said Hettie, almost crying. "How could I forget my sweetheart?"

"Shhh," Papa soothed. "We forget because it's been so long. But we will find him, I'm sure. The girl will find him, you'll see." But they all sat still and silent for a long time until Emily turned and left them. She did not know what was wrong, but she felt the sadness well out of the dollhouse like puffs of gray steam.

She trailed down to the second floor, where Gran was rummaging in a closet, murmuring to herself.

"Five woolen blankets, two down comforters, one..." She broke off as Emily stood beside her. "Hello, child, did you rescue that doll from the tree? I saw Mr. White brought his ladder over for you. Such a good neighbor."

"Yes, we rescued Violet, and she seemed to be happy; they all seemed to be happy. I made them tea for breakfast. I don't think they've ever had real tea before, Gran, and they were very cheered up."

"Mmmm," said Gran, still counting.

"I knew they were happy, Gran, the way you hear a faraway song in the air and can't quite name it. But then it suddenly got dark and gloomy in the dollhouse. I think they were sad, but..." She broke off and clapped her hands together. "Of course, I forgot! Walter."

"Which one is Walter again, dear?" asked Gran, tucking a golden blanket under a pile in the closet.

"The little boy doll they think someone took away. He's lost, and no one knows how to find him! I've got to get busy."

Emily went downstairs and stood in the door watching her sister grumble at a piece of the puzzle that wouldn't fit where she thought it should. It was just like Rose to keep trying to jam a piece into a space instead of setting it aside. Should she say anything to her sister about looking for Walter? Emily scratched her nose, thinking. No! Not after Rose had tossed Violet up in the tree yesterday!

When Rose grunted and threw the piece against the wall, Emily went out the front door. She would find Walter on her own. Going over to the butternut tree, she sat down. Had Alice put the dolls here long ago and left them out all night? Had some creature come and taken

Walter? If his shirt was soaked with milk, he would smell tasty to a fox or a porcupine or a raccoon. But maybe some*one* took him. Hettie spoke of a "little boy with a puffy nose" who never liked them. Who? Uncle Ted had a squat nose, and Uncle Edward had a red, angry face but not a puffy nose. Daddy? What did he look like when he was little?

Emily went back inside and found her grandmother in one of the upstairs bedrooms. "Gran?" Emily stood near her. Just being beside Gran calmed her and made her think that she *could* solve the mystery of Walter.

"Where are the pictures of your kids when they were young?"

"What do you want those for?" Gran murmured, peering through the window at a bluebird. "Look at that! Mr. White put up three bluebird houses in April, and they're all full, every last one of 'em!" She turned and smiled at Emily.

"I want to look at the photos because the dolls said a boy with a puffy nose didn't like them very much. Maybe he took Walter someplace and hid him."

"A boy with a puffy nose?" Gran said with dignity. "*I* never had a child with a puffy nose!"

"Well, maybe it looked that way to the dolls, Gran. Please help!"

"All right, come with me." Emily followed her into the wide hall, where a bench was next to a tall glass-fronted bookcase. Gran swung open the door and took out a black album.

"Sit down, child, sit down." She patted the bench. "Now, look at that!"

Emily peered at the page of photos; there was Daddy at the beach when he was two years old. A white floppy hat obscured his face. Did he have a puffy nose? Emily wondered.

"Here's your father, when he was five. That was the summer he got bit by a grass snake, and he never forgot it, either!" Emily looked at a photo of a bawling child, holding one hand in the other.

"Who took that, Gran? Weren't you running around trying to make him better?"

"Mmmm," Gran murmured, "we were. I think your grandfather took it; he just happened to have the camera out then."

They looked at other photos: of the family at the beach; of Christmases with children caught ripping open presents; of birthday parties; of weddings. All three of Grandma's little boys had puffy noses as far as Emily could tell. That didn't help her one bit. Emily stood up and dusted off her lap.

"Did you find what you were looking for?" Gran asked.

"Nope, but thanks for looking with me." Emily trailed to the window at the end of the hall and looked over the meadow that ran down to the woods. Walter could be anywhere, Emily thought—in the barn, in the meadow, in the woods outside. How will I *ever* find him?

A crow flew up from the woods, cawing. If I can't find Walter, Emily thought, the dolls will never be happy, not ever. And somehow it seemed to her that the happiness of the dolls was tied to her happiness—hers and maybe even Rose's. That they would never settle in and be a family until the dolls were a family again, too.

chapter 6

VIOLET WOKE to find her bed jolting. She slid to the bottom of her bed and cried out, "Mama, Papa! What's happening?"

"Where? What?" wailed Mama.

"Hold on, dear ones!" shouted Papa from downstairs.

The dollhouse lurched, and Violet heard the voices of the two girls outside.

"Careful! Watch the corner!"

"I'm holding the heavy side; you've got the light side."

"No I don't!"

"You do too!"

The dollhouse tilted to one side, and the birdcage fell on top of Violet's bed. "Peep?" said the bird.

"Peep yourself!" Violet said crossly, the covers over her mouth.

"Stop it, stop it!" a voice yelled outside the dollhouse. Violet thought it was Emily.

The other girl replied, "Don't be so fussy—they're only dolls. They can't get hurt!"

The dollhouse lurched again and suddenly thumped down. All the furniture stopped sliding about. Violet looked around. The bureau was pressed up against the foot of her bed. A picture of a ship now listed to its side and made Violet feel rather ill, as if she were on the boat itself, heeled over as great waves dashed them along.

"Oh," groaned William from next door. "I think my head is broken. Mama'll have to bind it up in brown paper and vinegar. Isn't that what they did to Jack when he fell down the hill?"

"What a mess, what wreckage!" called Papa. "I'm up-side down in the parlor. Where are you, Hettie?"

"I'm under the kitchen table, dear," said Mama in a brave I'm-determined-to-carry-on voice. "There's a pot on my head."

"That would account for the muffled sound of your voice," answered Papa. "I'm sure they'll set things to right in no time, Hettie."

"You hope!" said William.

Suddenly a great blue eye peered at them through the

windowpane. If Violet could have jumped and run, she would have. As it was, she pretended her eyes were closed and tried not to look. The eye came closer. It blinked.

"Yikes! It looks like a tornado got our dolls, Emily!"

Another eye, a gentle, soft brown, looked through at Violet. "Oh, dear, the poor things. Here, help me, Rose!"

Two warm hands reached in and took Violet from under the covers. "You sit here, Violet, while I fix things up. I don't know what happened—we tried to be careful, but that last attic stair and the curve at the bottom! We wanted to have you here, in the hallway, so we could play with you more."

Emily clucked her tongue and arranged Violet's room, setting the birdcage upright and putting the pictures all back to their positions on the wall. Rose reached in and picked up William.

The girl's hands smelled faintly of cookies and the smell made him hungry. Rose sat him against the wall of his room and began to pick up his furniture, singing tunelessly to herself.

"Bureau here, lamp there, rug here." She shook the blue rug in William's face, and he sneezed twice in a row. But she did not notice, for she was sneezing herself.

"It's still dusty, Em, even after all that cleaning we did."

"Maybe it was the rug, Rose," said Emily. She did not want to get in an argument with her sister this morning. She would not even ask Rose to stop calling her "Em."

She was enjoying the feeling of working together, like a piece of music with no out-of-tune notes. She hummed a fragment of melody to herself and Hettie cried out, "Oh, what is that? What is that heavenly sound?"

"Music, dear one," answered Papa. "One of the girls—I think she's called Emily—is singing."

Emily fixed the kitchen so all the cups were back on their shelves in the Welsh cupboard. Taking Hettie out from under the table, she pulled the pot from the doll's head and sat her at the table with a cup nearby.

"There, have some nice tea, Hettie, and you'll feel much better. You've had an upset," she said.

"Emily!" said Rose. "They don't feel things, you know—they're just plaster or wood or whatever they're made of."

"They do too feel things," Emily said stubbornly.

The dolls could sense the argument coming, as if a black, roiling cloud were rushing toward them. Soon the air was full of the girls' disagreement.

"No they don't!" declared Rose. "Only people have feelings."

"They have doll feelings," countered Emily.

"And what are *those*?" demanded Rose, sitting back on her heels. Her face was flushed.

"Well, if you ever *listened,* maybe you'd find out!" said Emily, pushing Hettie's teacup so hard the tea sloshed out onto the table.

Rose stood suddenly, and William slid onto the floor. "I'm sick of your talking like this, Emily! You're making it up! You pay more attention to these dolls than you do to me! What about *my* feelings?" Jerking her breath in, Rose ran out of the room. Emily heard a door slam a second later.

"Oh, my," she sighed. A tear rolled down one cheek. Then another.

Soon Hettie cried out, "She's soaking my best canary yellow silk, Arthur. What can I do?"

"Endure," answered Papa. "Just endure."

"Oh," sobbed Emily, "I'm so tired of arguing. Why can't we ever play without arguing?"

William said softly, "Because she won't forgive you for loving us, that's why. She wants you to love *her.*"

Emily picked up William and looked at him oddly. "Did you say something?"

But William did not answer. Dolls are not allowed to talk with humans, except in extreme cases. But what he could do was think. And his clear, sharp thought pierced Emily. *Love her, too.*

Startled, she set William down on his bed and blew her nose on her handkerchief. "Love," she murmured. "I don't know anything about love."

"Oh, yes, you do, dear," chided Hettie. "Your mother has loved you all these years, and your father and grandmother. You know about being hugged when you were little. You know how someone big held your hand so you wouldn't fall down at the curb. You know about warm, soft hands rubbing your back at night when you're sick and can't sleep."

"What's a curb?" whispered Violet.

"And you know about love that rests light as a blanket over every sleeping child. You just can't name it yet," Hettie finished.

Emily sighed and put the dolls back in their appointed places, shaking her head ever so slightly. Had she imagined those words in her brain, clear and bright, like little stars in the darkness of her head?

"What do dolls know about love?" she said out loud, and rose, going down the hall and disappearing from the dolls' view.

"What, indeed," said Papa. "They don't know, do they? They think we have no hearts. But we do."

If Papa could have torn open his purple smoking jacket right then and there, he would have done so. Instead he tapped his chest. "Inside, on the wood, they painted a red heart on the day I was made. You have one, too, don't you, dear?"

Hettie answered, "Of course! They put it there when I was made, too."

William did not say anything. His parents said hearts were painted on their chests, but in the times when Emily changed his shirt, he'd never seen anything on his chest.

"I have a heart," Violet said dramatically. "It was there in the wood before they even made me. It was carved into the tree by a little boy, long ago in a beech wood under the sunlight. That is why I know about love and must have it. It is part of my being."

"Our Violet," said Mama, smiling slightly.

Only William stayed silent, wondering what a heart was for—and if he didn't have one, how could he get one?

William

"WHAT IS a heart?" William asked himself softly. Was it a bump on your body, he wondered, sucking on the tiny pencil Emily had given him. He had tried drawing, but the lines he made were all wobbly and shivery, for he had trouble grasping the slim pencil. His porcelain fingers were stiff and did not move easily.

Maybe a heart was something that grew. Once William remembered seeing a new plant popping out of the ground. Alice had left him under the butternut tree, and he was outside for a night and a morning before she remembered him. He had watched a tiny green nub thrust out of the earth and waver upward toward his knee.

Is a heart green? William asked himself. But it couldn't grow; otherwise how could it stay in your chest? And Papa had said his heart was red.

"Violet?" William called out. He could hear her tuneless humming next door, like the drone of a bee.

"Mmmm," she hummed.

"What is a heart?" he asked.

"Oh, William, you know what a heart is!"

"No, I don't. If I did, I wouldn't be asking you, would I? I remember that the minister with the purple voice once talked about them. He lived in that cold building Alice took me to, remember? He said something about laws being written on our hearts. But I didn't know what that meant. I still don't!" He threw his pencil across the room. He didn't want to draw. He wanted to leap and run and follow butterflies in the sun and go fishing. He would put a line into a rippling stream and catch a silver fish. Then Mama would cook it up on the stove.

"That kind of heart is something people have. Their hearts are big and thumping, and if they don't work the people die," said Violet.

"They die?" William said. "What is that?"

"I heard Papa talking about it once; I think your legs and arms fall off your body, and you don't work anymore."

"Ugh!" exclaimed William. "I'm glad I'm a doll and not a human!"

"Me, too. But William, our hearts are painted on wood and can never die. They are shaped a bit like a

45

circle with two bumps on top, and they narrow to a point on the bottom. The best kinds are red."

"Like candy?" William asked doubtfully. He'd once smelled a piece of candy in Alice's pocket.

"Maybe a bit like candy, but much better, William."

"But what good is a heart?" wailed William. He wanted one now, right this minute.

"It is for loving," Violet said.

It was better than candy. Without one, people died. They had to be red. They were like circles with bumps on the top. William tried tracing that shape on his blue shirt, but his fingers snagged in the buttonholes. How would he ever get a heart? He couldn't give one to himself. Someone else would have to give it to him, but who? Emily? The girl who sneezed? The little old lady with silver hair? Once there had been a boy with a puffy nose, but he had disappeared, as all boys do.

William sank back against his chair, pretending to read the little book Emily had put on his desk. He wanted to look earnest when she came to play. He wanted to look like the sort of doll who deserved a heart.

chapter 7

ROSE SAT in a hard chair and looked at everyone busy fixing up the dollhouse. Emily and her mother were cutting out bits of material for curtains and rugs while Gran seamed them up on her sewing machine. When they were done, Gran handed them back to Emily to sew fringe along the edges. There were purple rugs, a pair of green curtains, and a rug of a rather strange flowered material.

"Violet will like this," Emily said happily as she sewed. "It's romantic."

"Mmmm, she will, dear," agreed Gran, bent over her machine.

"This is lovely cloth," said Mother as she sat and snipped some red fabric. "What is it from?"

"Oh, some old chair Father and I used to have," Gran said. "It was a William Morris chair, actually, quite lovely but not very comfortable. It looked very elegant in that covering."

"What happened to it?" Mother asked. From a slight tightening around her lips, Rose knew Mother wished she had that chair. She loved old, beautiful things.

"I think Alice has it, Marge. Yes, I'm sure she does." Gran hummed to herself, feeding the material slowly and surely beneath the needle.

Mother pursed her lips, as if Alice always got the good things from Grandmother's house and she and Dad only got leftovers. It surprised Rose to see her mother that way, as if she and Alice were fighting over Gran's furniture the way Rose and Emily fought over the dollhouse.

"I like this!" Emily said, sucking on her underlip as she sewed gold fringe onto a purple rug. "This will make Papa happy, and Hettie loves rich-looking things."

Mother looked over at Gran, who did not respond. Rose thought her mother was amused at Emily's fantasy and wanted Gran to be amused, too. Instead Rose shared a smile with Mother and said, "Emily's made up a lot of stories about the dollhouse."

Gran stopped feeding the material under the needle. "Who says they're made up, Rose?"

Rose stammered, "Well, they m-m-must be, mustn't

they? Dolls don't care about rugs, and how could they be happy? They're just wood and whatever it is their heads are made of." She chewed on her thumbnail.

"How do you know?" asked Gran quietly.

"I used to think my dolls talked at night after I turned out all the lights," Mother said. "Sometimes I stayed up late, pretending to be asleep, hoping I would hear them."

"Oh, did you?" Emily said happily. "That's nice."

Mother smiled and nodded.

"Were your dolls ever sad, Mother? Our dolls are. They can't find Walter, and everyone's terribly upset about it. I wish I could help, but I don't seem to be able to." Emily frowned and untied a knot in the fringe.

Rose clenched her hands. Emily's fingers were swift and capable, not clumsy and round like hers. Her chest began to feel hot and tight. Everyone was settling in, everyone except her.

"Who's Walter, and what happened to him?" Mother asked, whipping fine stitches along a curtain hem.

"Someone took him, or maybe a fox got him. He's the littlest doll. The problem is he could be anywhere!" Emily sighed and stared out the window.

"That's too bad, dear," said Mother, and Rose knew that she did not believe Emily. It made her chest feel a little less tight.

She laughed harshly. "How could a fox take a doll, Em? What an imagination you have!" She stood and began to swing her leg back and forth, rather close to Emily.

Gran looked up at her. "Dolls can get lost just like children get lost, Rose."

It was too much! Rose thought. Everyone was taking Emily's side! She strode to the door and said, "I'm sick of dolls," leaving before any words could follow her. But still Rose listened, hoping someone would call out, "Oh, Rose, come back—we know how you feel." But no one spoke. The hall was empty and silent. Daddy was off on a walk somewhere, trying to follow the doctor's orders to walk for an hour each day.

Rose went upstairs slowly, dragging her feet. How did Emily know so much about the dolls? Did Gran believe in them, too? She walked to the end of the hall and sat in front of the dollhouse. Violet was perched on her bed, looking at the canary in the cage. Her face was quiet and sweet, like the heroine in a novel—the kind that was meant to improve your morals, Rose thought. William was in the bedroom next door, seated at a tiny desk with a sheet of paper spread out. Emily thought he was interested in birds and might like to draw them.

Rose breathed heavily through her nose and William shivered. "She's up to no good, Violet, mark my words. The righteous shall be forsaken!" he said dramatically.

"Oh, pooh," sniffed Violet. "She's just in a bad mood—nothing to worry about."

But Papa saw the dangerous glint in Rose's eyes. Shifting nervously on the horsehair sofa, he warned, "She looks angry, Hettie. I can feel it coming out of her in great red waves. If we get separated, remember to call each other so we'll know where we are."

50

As Rose stared at the dolls, she saw the quiet, ordered way they fit into their house, the way they sat in their neat clothes with all their things about them. And it seemed to her that they had everything she did not have: an ordered life, love, safety, and the chance of happiness. Her life felt like a box being unpacked with bits and pieces everywhere and nothing in its place. Her clothes were tight and ill-fitting. All the things she loved were far away. She stared at Violet. Violet looked back with her cornflower blue eyes.

Rose hated everything about Violet—her sweet prettiness, her tiny feet in the black slippers, the way her blond hair lay in neat coils along her tiny, wooden shoulders. Suddenly she seized the doll and stuffed her in the pocket of her shorts. Then Rose folded a tiny blanket, put it under the covers of Violet's bed, and ran downstairs.

"Help!" called Violet. "Emily, help! Papa, Mama, William!"

Rose darted out the door, swung her leg over her bicycle, and sped down the drive onto the tarred road. She did not know where she was going; she just had to get away from the dollhouse. The wind flew in her face, stinging her eyes. Her legs pumped the pedals, sending her faster and faster downhill.

Inside Rose's pocket, Violet was aware of air rushing by. Through a hole in the material, she saw the black road whizzing beneath her. It made her dizzy. As the bumps heaved her from side to side in the pocket, she began to feel queasy and ill. After a time the jostling slowed, the bike wheeled over one great bump, and then over something that crackled and popped. They stopped. The girl got off the bicycle and walked; Violet could see grass through the hole in the pocket. They went a little ways, and Violet saw something gray and hard like a rock.

Sitting down on the grass, Rose took Violet out of her pocket. Sunlight washed over the doll's face, sweet and welcome after the darkness.

"Here. You are a romantic; Emily says so. You can sit here and be romantic about all these people who died. You can cry over them and sing them songs." Her voice was hard and angry.

Rose sat Violet against a hard slab of rock that shone in the sunlight. Deep lines were cut in its surface, and rainwater had caught in some of them. A spider crawled out of one of the lines and crept up her dress.

"Oh!" shrieked Violet. "I hate spiders! Get off me!" The spider hurried to the edge of her green dress and disappeared. Violet looked around as Rose mounted her bicycle and pedaled away. A bluebird swooped low and perched in a sweet-smelling bush nearby. It cocked its head and eyed her curiously.

"Peep?"

"Peep, yourself!" Violet answered, wanting to cry. "Why me? Why does that girl always pick on me? First the butternut tree, now this, whatever this is." She sat for a while and tried to think. Papa had said to call each other if they were separated. She concentrated very hard and thought, sending him a picture of where she was—

tidy green grass covered with regular blocks of gray rock with some kind of carved letters on them. Flowers stood in front of some of the stones. She had no idea where she was.

In the dollhouse Papa came to attention. "I've got a picture, Hettie, a picture from Violet."

He paused and Hettie cried out, "Where, Arthur, where is she?"

"Green grass," he muttered, "lots of gray stones marching along, a bluebird, some flowers. I don't know!" he said in an exasperated voice.

Upstairs William had the same picture in his head of grass with the carved rocks on its surface. Suddenly he said, "Oh, I've seen that before. I went there once with Alice, in her pocket. It's . . . It's . . ." He fumbled with the words.

"What?" Hettie called from downstairs. "What is it, William?"

William sighed. Dredging up the name was like trying to find a pair of boots in a jumbled, dark cupboard. "It is," he said slowly, "a . . . sad place. But I forget the name."

Papa slumped against the purple horsehair sofa. "A sad place! That doesn't help, William! How will we find her? How will Emily find her?"

"We could put pictures in her head," answered William. "I think I can do that."

"Oh, try," cried Hettie, "dear William, try! I cannot bear it if I lose *two* of my children!"

"There, there," Papa soothed, "everything will be all

right, Hettie. Remember, happiness is in store for us. I've seen it over the dollhouse, like stars."

Hettie wanted to say "Pshaw!" but felt it would be too rude and unkind. He was trying to cheer them up, but it was no use. What was the point of being awake, Hettie wondered, if all they got was sorrow and pain?

chapter 8

WHEN EMILY went upstairs with the new curtains and rugs in her hands, she was humming. The dollhouse gleamed in the late afternoon sun. Everything looked ordered and perfect. Kneeling down, she put the purple rug with the gold fringe on the parlor floor.

"This is for you, Hettie. I think purple is your favorite color."

"It is," Hettie answered. "Light purple to a deep mauve, I love them all. And sometimes there is a color blue, like a deep northern lake, that makes me feel quite peaceful."

Emily sang, fixing the red curtains over the windows. It looked like a real house; it looked like the sort of place where people would read books, have conversations, disagree, make up, and sit at the table for tea.

Time slipped by and before she knew it, Emily heard Mother calling her to supper. Where was Rose? It was odd the way she had disappeared. Just before she went downstairs, Emily tweaked the covers of Violet's bed.

"Time to wake up. Come see all the changes I've made." She reached in to pull out the doll, but Violet was gone. In her place was a wadded-up blanket from another bed.

Emily raced to the dining room and stood, panting, in front of Rose's place. Her sister looked curiously subdued, sitting quietly in her chair.

"All right, where is she?"

"Where's who?" Rose did not lift her head.

"You know who's missing! Where did you take her? Back to the butternut tree or somewhere else this time?" Emily jammed her hands on her hips.

Gran looked at Emily over her gold spectacles. "Girls, girls, not at the supper table. Sit down, eat dinner, and work it out after we're all done. No one wants to hear you arguing."

"Amen," said Daddy, cutting his chicken with quick, sharp jabs. "There's been enough arguing between you two to last me a year."

"Ever since we left the city," said Mother, "you've been at each other like cats and dogs."

Words bunched behind Emily's lips, but she did not

let them out. Even Rose was silent, putting chicken into her mouth automatically and not looking up.

It was not until after supper, when the dishes were done and the rest of the family was on the front porch drinking coffee, that Emily had a chance to talk to Rose. She had her hand in the cookie jar when Emily came up to her.

"Where is she?" Emily demanded.

"Where's who?" Rose said absently, fiddling with the big oatmeal cookies Gran had made earlier that day. They were especially nice, with raisins bulging out of the sides and little chunks of hard brown sugar your teeth crunched on. Rose had already had two, but somehow she still felt empty.

Emily shook her arm. "Violet, that's who! Where did you take her? I *know* you took her because there was that rolled-up blanket under her covers. The dolls wouldn't do that. Dolls can't lie—did you know that?"

Rose turned, stuffing the last cookie into her mouth. "Don't be silly, Em. Dolls can't talk, so they can't tell the truth *or* lie, can they!" She seemed pleased with her reasoning and smiled, one cheek puffed out to the side.

"Oooh! I could hit you! There you are, with your mouth *full* of the last cookie—yes, I know it's the last one, you greedy-guts—and talking about telling the truth after stealing one of our dolls!"

"Well," Rose said, swallowing the last of the cookie and sitting down at the table. "Then I didn't steal her, did I, if she's ours? You can't steal what belongs to you."

Emily seized Rose's arm and twisted it up behind her.

57

Her sister shrieked. Emily put her mouth very close to Rose's ear and hissed, "Either you tell me where she is, or I will twist this arm until it breaks!"

Emily couldn't believe she was being so fierce. She was the one who never hit back; she was the one who ran off rather than get in another fight. But she felt she would do anything for Violet. As she jerked Rose's arm tighter, her sister began to cry.

"All right, all right! She's in the graveyard, and if you think I'm going to tell you where, you're even stupider than I think you are!" When Emily loosened her grip for a second, Rose jumped up and darted through the door, across the lawn. Emily could hear her crying—great, ragged gulps of sound that lurched through the darkening air. It made her feel even worse. What was the point of beating somebody if they cried like that?

A hand on her shoulder startled her.

"What's wrong with you two? Is this the same argument?" came Gran's soft voice.

Emily leaned back against her. "She took Violet, Gran, the one who loves flowers. And she left her in the graveyard somewhere! What if something comes and eats her at night? Or takes her away and loses her, like Walter!" She turned and buried her head in Gran's shoulder.

Gran patted her back, murmuring, "Hush, now, hush, everything's going to be all right. A little night air never hurt anybody, least of all Violet. She's a great deal hardier than you think she is." She stroked Emily's back. "When we go to get her tomorrow morning, you'll find that she's none the worse for wear. If her clothes are damp from the dew, we'll just dry them."

Emily sniffed and blew her nose on the handkerchief Gran offered. It had little purple violets embroidered in the corner. "I wish...," she started.

"I wish you two could stop arguing so much," Gran interrupted. "Isn't that what you were going to say, too? You never used to fight like this. Doesn't it hurt your stomach?"

Emily nodded mutely.

"What do you think you can do about it?" Gran asked, sitting and pulling Emily down beside her. It was almost completely dark outside now, and Emily saw her father switching on the porch light.

She shook her head. "I don't know, Gran; I really don't. I thought the dollhouse would be something we could work on together, and it would sort of join us up...like a tune." She waved her hand. "But it's almost made things worse!"

"It's harder for Rose than it is for you," Gran said.

"What is?" Emily took a deep breath.

"Leaving home. She's like a cat who doesn't like change."

Emily did not answer, staring out into the dark where the pine trees stood up like smudged figures of giant animals, swaying in the wind. She couldn't hear Rose. She imagined her outside, huddling under the butternut tree, still crying. Suddenly she got up.

"Thanks, Gran, thanks for listening. I'm going out there right now."

"That's my girl. When there's a battle, you know, someone has to be the peacemaker."

Emily walked down the front steps, across the tree shadows on the lawn to the butternut tree. At first she did not see Rose. But after a time she heard a soft sniff and turned to see a blacker patch near the trunk.

"Rose, it's me. Come on in; don't stay out here in the dark."

There was another sniff, then a cough.

Emily crouched beside her. Rose was all scrunched up, her head plunged between her knees, hair covering her face.

"Come on—let's go in." She touched her sister's knee.

Rose did not answer but stood up, swaying slightly. In a shaft of light from the porch, Emily saw that her sister's face was swollen and red. "Don't you hate arguing?" Emily said, holding out her arm. "Doesn't it make your stomach feel awful?

Rose stumbled on the lawn and clutched Emily's arm. "Yes, it does," she muttered, so quietly that Emily almost didn't hear her. "It's just that everything's all changed, and none of our friends are here, and the air smells different, and none of the sounds are the same, and even the sky looks different. It's not home!" She began to cry again, soft gulps of sound.

"I know, I know," Emily murmured. She repeated something she'd heard her mother say, "Too many changes all at once. Maybe," she said, fumbling for the words as they neared the front steps, "maybe if we make a home for the dolls..." She paused.

Rose stopped on the bottom step and turned to her. "You think *that* will make *this* a home for us?"

Emily nodded. "It might *help.*"

Rose did not answer, and just gave a bleak look as she pushed through the kitchen door.

Violet

VIOLET LEANED BACK against the hard
stone. She wished she could get up and wander around,
although walking was almost impossible for her—her legs
were still too stiff. But she hated just sitting here, waiting
to be found. Although she wiggled and stretched as hard
as she could, Violet sank lower into the grass. Now her
head looked up at the sky, and she could not see what
was coming across the grass.

"Silly," she told herself sternly. If she had a governess—she'd heard about them once in a story—the

governess would tell her to keep her chin up and be brave. Maybe even sing some rousing tunes.

She hummed to herself, something Mama sang at times. It went, "Oh, the noble Duke of York," and had something about his marching his men up to the top of the hill and down again. Violet didn't have a clue what it meant, but it was a gay, brave tune, the sort of thing to keep her spirits up.

Violet looked down at her green dress, remembering the day her heart had been painted on her chest. The dollmaker was humming, and his hand had moved surely and swiftly over her.

"You have a big heart, girl doll," he had said. "The log we made you from had a heart carved into it, all the way through the bark."

Violet tried to remember more about when she was made. The first time she knew she was alive was when someone joined all her limbs together and made them swing back and forth. Motion! Air on her body! Then a warm hand painted blue eyes and a red mouth on her face. She saw shiny eyeglasses and heard someone talking. It was then her heart was painted on. The man glued blond hair to her head, then fitted her with a silk dress and tiny soft slippers. She had felt cared for, special.

Now, in the graveyard, the light dimmed and a fine dew settled on Violet. "My dress," she moaned, "my new green dress." Just then a big, fat bug waddled up to her and touched her skirt with its feelers.

"Get off!" screamed Violet. "Go away, you—you

insect!" The astonished bug reared back and galloped away as fast as he could go. As she watched him disappear, she saw colors laid like scarves at the edge of the sky. "I am beginning to know this quite well," sighed Violet. "First it is pink, then purple, sometimes a yellow flush along the tops of the hills. Finally everything becomes gray, then black. And last, the stars come out."

Later Violet looked up. The stars seemed friendly, if far away. The same points of light were above her family at home. She could wish on them. Her wish was hard and bright, spinning out over the grass, up the road, and through the open window to Emily, asleep in her bed. The wish circled into Emily's curved ear.

Come find me, soon. I'm against a stone. Come find me, Emily! In her dream, Emily twitched and sighed, searching and searching for her doll.

Then a weasel scampered up, nudging its nose against the edge of Violet's dress. It sniffed and seized the cloth in its sharp teeth.

"Go away!" shrieked Violet. But the weasel, after one surprised glance, did not leave. It tugged and dragged her over the grass until it stopped. Maybe she didn't smell red enough; didn't have enough heat to eat.

Violet lay in the grass, her eyes open to the stars. Sorrow wrapped her like a blanket. *If ever I get back to my home again,* she thought, *I will love you, Emily, until you die. I will love your children and your children's children, and I will write their names on my heart.*

In bed Emily stirred, murmured "heart," and snuggled back to sleep again.

chapter 9

EMILY ROSE EARLY the next day. She peered into the dollhouse on her way down the hall. It stood under the window, the one that overlooked the road and the two great maple trees at its edge. All the dolls were lying in bed, covers up to their chins. Although their eyes were not closed, they seemed asleep to Emily, with a faraway look on their faces. Papa seemed serious and sad. William lay on the bed with the covers thrown back, as if he'd woken from a bad dream and pushed them away. And Hettie had the look of someone who has cried out all her tears and is merely exhausted.

But dolls don't cry, Emily thought; dolls can't be sad. That's what her sister would say, and that's why she wouldn't ask Rose to come find Violet.

"It's all right. I'll find Violet—don't worry," Emily whispered the words over the dollhouse, hoping that they might hear her in their sleep and be comforted when they woke.

She tiptoed downstairs. The sun was just coming up over the blue hill outside the window. No one was awake. There was no smell of coffee from the kitchen, no warm scent of bread toasting. Emily had never thought before how empty and lonely a house was with no smells in it. Rubbing her nose, she threw on her windbreaker and wheeled her bicycle out of the back shed. Breakfast would come after she had found Violet.

She rode down the hill to the cemetery, over gravel that popped and crackled under her tires. Sighing, she dismounted and laid her bicycle on the grass. How would she ever find Violet? She could be anywhere in the grave-yard, leaning against a stone, up in a tree, anywhere.

"I guess I just have to start somewhere," she spoke aloud to comfort herself. "Why not start at the very be-ginning of the cemetery and divide it up into squares, taking them one at a time."

Farther down in the graveyard, Violet woke to the sound of robins and busy insects. Beside her a worm squooged through the earth, poking out a load of soil and then its pink, naked head.

"Oh!" said Violet. "What do *you* want? Would you like to drag me around, too? Would you like to nibble my dress? Go ahead! I'm just a doll." Violet stared angrily as the worm looked at her in mute surprise and pulled its head back underground. She tugged stiffly at her new green dress. It had been so pretty the day before, the way it lay in soft folds about her body. The sunlight had caught in the fabric just as light shone on leaves, Violet thought. And when Emily had moved her, the dress had rustled slightly, like the sea.

Leaning her head back against the hard stone where the weasel had left her, Violet looked up at the sky. A crow flew across, cawing busily. A bluejay called from a near pine. Things moved in the grass to her side, but she did not want to look. Instead she imagined what her family was doing at home in the dollhouse. Papa would be sleeping in bed, his half-finished book propped on his knees. He had decided to improve his mind, and he was reading the book about birds Emily had made for William.

"It's important to *know* things," he had declared yesterday.

Mama would be worrying about her, Violet knew. She imagined how Mama would feel if *two* of her children were lost. Where was Walter? Violet wondered. What if he was here nearby, under a stone or in the woods? She would try calling to him.

Walter, where are you? Walter, can you hear me? I am near you, out in the world, on top of the green and under the blue. Are you out here, too? Though Violet sent her thoughts spinning out like bright globes, Walter did not hear. Asleep in the tunnel in the woods, he did not even stir when the words circled into his ears.

Violet sighed and thought of Emily. *Emily, come find me. I am somewhere outside on green grass with stones all around.* She looked up and saw something that looked like a giant stone table. That's silly, she thought, but kept the picture in her mind. *I am here, Emily. Come find me, and I will love you forever.*

In the middle of the graveyard, Emily sat and bunched her knees under her chin. She had been looking for more than an hour, checking each stone, peering under the pine branches in log planters and fake geraniums. Where *was* Violet? She didn't think Hettie could stand it, having two children gone. But, as Emily sat, she felt something tapping inside her head, almost as if a tiny hand knocked there.

Four stone legs with a flat top. A picture came into her head. Something like a table with Violet nearby.

Emily jumped up. It must be Violet talking to her! Or *thinking* to her. She ran down the gravel road, searching from side to side. She passed a huge gray tower with a monstrous ball on top and a group of tiny stones set into the grass like a row of white teeth. Must be children, she thought. Then around the curve, by the caretaker's shed, she saw a large, flat stone table. She ran to it and knelt down. On the far side of the monument, nestled among the long grasses, was the doll.

"Oh, Violet, *here* you are!" She picked her up gently

and hugged her. Taking out her handkerchief, Emily wiped the doll's face, eyes, and dress. "Too bad, your dress got all wet. But don't worry—I'll fix that when we get home." She tucked Violet in her pocket and ran back down the lane.

"It's too bad we can't give you a bath; that's what you really need. I bet you got cold out there all night. I'm really sorry Rose left you there. I know it was a mean thing to do, but you know how people are when they're sad. She didn't *mean* to be mean."

Violet breathed in the scent of chewing gum and freshly washed clothes. She felt Emily's warm legs pumping up and down. The warmth comforted her. *Soon, I'll be home soon, and I will love you forever, Emily.*

An elderly man planting geraniums looked up as Emily hurried past. She didn't see the questioning look he gave her as she talked to the doll. She was too intent on getting Violet home and drying her off.

"And Gran can make you a new dress out of green cloth if this one's ruined, so don't worry," Emily said as she mounted her bike and turned onto the road. A tiny thread of song started in her throat. She had found Violet all by herself without any more arguments with Rose. What was it Gran had said last night? "Someone has to be the peacemaker." And when she got home, she would not say one *word* that might blame Rose. In some way Emily felt if they could just stop arguing, they could make a home.

chapter 10

IT'S NOT FAIR," William exclaimed from the purple sofa. He stared at Violet, recently rescued from the graveyard and now in her old yellow dress.

"*You* always have the adventures. *You* always go outside. I've never ridden on a bike, not once, not ever!" He leaned against the flowered cushions of the sofa.

"You wouldn't want my adventure," Violet said in a low voice. "It was terrible."

"Hush, William," Hettie soothed. "I'm sure you'll have your turn. Maybe that big girl—is Rose her name? In fact,

I think that's her right now, crouching outside our house. Maybe she will be mad at *you* next time and fling you off into the forest."

William looked out and saw the round pink face of the girl with the dent in her chin. Rose, her name was. "I don't *want* to be flung into the forest, Mama, just let outside for a little adventure, a little sunshine. What I really want to do is go fishing, just once in my life. Is that too much to ask?"

Rose stared at the dolls. They seemed animated somehow, almost as if they were talking together. She shook her head; that would be impossible. But somehow, she stayed fixed in front of the dollhouse, feeling guilty about what she had done to Violet yesterday and surprised that Emily had said nothing when she brought Violet home.

Papa wanted to stick his hands in his pockets but knew he could not move while the child was there. "No, William, it isn't too much to ask to go fishing. But asking won't do us much good, will it? They do with us what they will, and we just have to put up with it."

"That's the trouble!" William shouted. "I am tired of being a doll. I want to run and jump; I want to *do* things, not just sit here all my life. And I want a heart," he whispered, so softly no one heard.

"Well," Papa said calmly, "if you were alive like *them*, you couldn't be a boy forever."

"I couldn't?" William's eyes almost blinked. "What would happen to me?"

"Your legs would grow, your arms would get longer,

your face would grow stubbly black hair on it, your voice would get lower, and you would become a man. I know; I've seen it happen."

"Ugh!" William shuddered. "Black bristly hair, you said?"

"Mmm-hmm. You wouldn't play anymore—I'm not sure about all the details—and then one day you would die."

"*Die?* Oh, I remember Violet telling me that word."

"Your heart stops beating. Your arms stop working. And you—you"—Papa waved his arm vaguely—"fall over and break into pieces. And never get up again."

"My, my, I, for one, am happy I am a doll," Violet said strongly. "I wouldn't want hair on *my* face." She smoothed its curves gently and gave a complacent smile. "And I don't like that part about breaking into pieces at all!"

"Of course," Hettie put in gently, "that can happen to dolls as well, dear."

"What can, Mama?" Violet plucked fretfully at her old dress.

Rose, crouching nearby, suddenly stiffened. The thought had come unbidden into her mind: *I wish I had my new dress back. I hate this color, and I hate being left out at night!* For one awful moment, Rose felt something of what Violet had felt last night: darkness coming down like a suffocating blanket; frightening creatures scurrying through the grass.

Her face paled and she stood up, steadying herself on

the dollhouse roof. "I must be getting sick," Rose said loudly, in a determined voice. "Dreams, fever dreams, that's it!" And she went into her room to lie down.

"What can happen to dolls, Mama?" Violet repeated, wondering why the girl had gone away.

"Falling into pieces and never getting up again. In fact, that is just what I'm afraid has happened to our Walter. What if his arms came off, Arthur? What if his legs have fallen off and his feet? Can he be put back together?" Hettie uttered a low moan.

Papa wanted to come and sit beside her on the sofa, but he remembered the rule: Dolls must not change the positions they've been left in by their people. So he waved an arm at Hettie and smiled encouragingly. "If Walter has started to fall apart, he can be put back together again. Remember: He is made out of porcelain, not just his face, hands, and feet. He can be fixed with glue and string, glue and string."

They repeated it softly, as if it were a chant inside a church. "Glue and string, glue and string."

"I wonder where Walter is?" Violet asked.

"Under the sky," replied William, wishing he could see the sun and moon again.

"Inside the forest," said Papa, thinking of Walter's clothes moldering away into shreds.

"We *must* find Walter before he falls to pieces!" Hettie clutched her hands together.

"We must lead him out of the valley of the shadow of death," William intoned.

"William!" snapped Papa. "Stop speaking like that. It doesn't help, not at all. Let's put our heads together and think. Think!"

Inside Violet's head, thoughts caromed around like balls, knocking against the sides of her head. Call to him, she thought.

Papa thought, We must shake him awake somehow.

Hettie wondered, If he could only hear us, would that mean he's all right?

And William repeated, to himself, Lead him out of the valley of the shadow of death.

Hettie said slowly, "We just haven't been trying hard enough. All we've done is call gently to him. What if we *yell* to him and *sing* to him, and make our wishes so hard and strong that they knock against his head until he wakes up?"

"Yes," said Papa, "that's it, Hettie. All together, let's sing and yell until he *has* to hear us!"

"All right," William said. "I'm ready."

"Ready," echoed Violet.

"On the count of three, *wish* him to be awake and to look through his eyes. On the next count of three, *yell* together, and on the next count of three, *sing* together." Papa leaned forward eagerly.

"On the count of three, let's say, 'Walter, wake up! Look through your eyes and be alive.'"

Walter, wake up! Look through your eyes and be alive. Walter, wake up!

Then Papa said, "Next, we yell. One, two, three!"

WALTER, WAKE UP! LOOK THROUGH YOUR
EYES AND BE ALIVE. WALTER, WAKE UP!

Something fluttered on the sunbeam, some faint response like a whisper from a deep, dark cellar, as if a long-forgotten prisoner had whispered his name into the blackness.

"Oh!" Hettie shrieked. "I think he said something."

"All right, here we go; try again. This time we *sing* on the count of three."

"Sing what?" Violet asked sharply.

"What did you used to sing to him, dear?" Hettie asked.

" 'Rockabye, Baby,' " answered Violet.

"Then that's what we will do," said Papa. "One, two, three!"

Rockabye, baby, on the tree top; when the wind blows the cradle will rock; when the bough breaks the cradle will fall, and DOWN will come baby, cradle, and all. Walter, wake up, wake up!

Their sharp, hard wishes spun out over the grass, through the green leaves, down the dark hole to where Walter lay. Their thoughts pounded on his head, again and again. One thought wormed its way into his ear and squiggled down inside his body, making him twitch and squirm. And for one moment he saw through his left eye. Slowly, reluctantly, he saw darkness, light, and a soft green wash beyond the darkness.

"Mmmmmm, trees," he murmured.

Hettie twisted her hands. "Did anyone else hear that? A tiny sound, like a child stirring?"

For a moment the warmth of the earth seeped into Walter's shoulder. He twitched and burrowed deeper into the dream he had been in for so many years.

"I thought I heard a little sound," Papa said faintly.

"Me, too," William said. "Did he say 'trees'?"

"I did not hear one thing," declared Violet.

William glared at her. "Trust you to spoil it, Violet!"

"Hush!" commanded Papa. "Let's listen again. Quiet, everyone!" They waited in silence, waiting for some signal from their lost child, some word that he was still alive. But nothing more came.

"Still," Hettie said, "I heard him, Arthur. I *did*! He's going to be all right—if we can only find him. Do you think he's in the woods?"

"We *will* find Walter, my dear," Papa assured her. "I am sure of it."

chapter 11

WHAT HAPPENED?" Emily knelt in front of the dollhouse the next day. "You look excited."

She couldn't be quite sure, but Hettie's face had a glow to it, like a small sun. Did Papa's mustache curve up at the corners? Maybe they were just happy to be all clean and together again in their house. Or . . .

"Did you hear something from Walter?" she whispered to Violet.

"What are you doing?"

Emily jumped as Rose came up and knelt on the floor.

"Nothing, nothing." Then she thought she might share this with Rose; it was part of trying to make a settled family—one for the dolls, one for them. "Don't you think they look happy, Rose? Look at Papa and Hettie."

"How could they be happy?" Rose said, more out of habit than anything else. She didn't want to remember those words in her mind yesterday, that sense of Violet's unhappiness.

"I think they've been trying to find Walter, and maybe they know something," Emily replied.

Rose coughed and rubbed her nose. "You know, Violet hates that old dress."

"She does?" Emily stared at her sister in surprise. How did she know *that*? Had the dolls been talking to her—in a dream?

"Yes, she does. Gran's fixing her a new one, isn't she?"

Worry puckered Rose's forehead, and Emily hastened to say, "Of course she is. Violet will be just fine, and so will her dress."

"Good," Rose sighed. Then she noticed William. He seemed to have an eager look on his face, as if he expected something wonderful to happen. "I wonder what he wants?" she asked. "Doesn't he look as if he wants to go somewhere or do something, Emily?"

Her sister grinned. "Yes, he does." This must be it; the dolls were beginning to get to Rose. She was changing.

William looked up at the girl with the pink face and the dent in her chin. Maybe she wasn't so bad after all.

Hadn't she just asked what he wanted? "There's hope for the fallen," he murmured to Violet. "I'm going to try to tell her what I want."

Fishing, he thought, sending out words to Rose. *I want to catch a tiny silver fish for Mama.*

The thought spun into Rose's head and knocked against her brain. *Fishing*—the word bounced around inside. She gasped and looked at William. Dolls can't talk, she reminded herself in a loud inside voice. Dolls can't have wishes!

"I think all the dolls want things, Rose," Emily said, settling Violet against the sofa cushions. "I know Hettie wants to find Walter—they *all* want to find Walter—and Violet wants to put him on her lap and sing lullabies."

"Violet wants that? How do you know?" Rose demanded.

"She told me in a dream, remember?"

Frightened by too many changes all at once, Rose snapped, "That dream! Probably something you ate. You have to have a brain and a heart to want something, Em."

William shouted up at Rose, "I *do* have a brain, whatever that is, and I would have a heart if I could," he finished sadly.

Rose stared back at him, frowning. Somehow, without her wishing it, he was no longer jointed wood covered with cloth. Somehow the bright red cheeks and grinning mouth belonged to something alive. She took a deep breath and wiped her forehead.

Emily gave her one last curious look and went back

downstairs. She was not going to argue with her sister about the dolls or what they wanted. Rose would have to figure it out on her own.

"Be careful!" warned Papa, staring up at Rose. "She's the one with the temper. Remember to keep in touch in case anything happens!"

William shrieked as Rose reached out and took him gently between her thumb and front finger.

"Don't worry," she said softly, and put him in her shorts pocket and ran downstairs.

"Good-bye, good-bye, my family!" shouted William. The faint cries of the dolls followed him downstairs.

Rose clattered into the kitchen and said, "Gran, is there any string in your back shed?"

Everyone was sitting around the table, eating egg-salad sandwiches. "Yes, honey, there's some in a bucket out back. You'll find it. Your grandpa put labels on everything. How about a sandwich, Rose?" Gran asked.

"Not now, Gran. Can I have it later, please?"

"All right—just this once," Mother answered. "Are you off on an expedition?"

"Can I go, too?" Emily asked, half rising from her chair.

"No, no!" Rose flapped her hand at Emily. "I'm not going anywhere. I just don't . . . don't feel like eating right now."

Grabbing a piece of cheese, she ran through the connecting door to the back shed. Reaching up to a high shelf, she found the white bucket labeled TWINE AND STRING. She took it down and used Gran's garden scissors to cut two different lengths. Then she ran out the back door to the lilac grove, where she found two dry sticks to use for fishing poles; one long one for her, a tiny one for William.

She did everything quickly, not wanting Emily to see her or ask questions. I must be going crazy, she thought. I won't tell anyone what I'm doing.

"Now," she whispered, "I've got two fishing poles— one for you, one for me, William."

William stirred in her pocket, terrified. Where was she taking him? Was Rose going to fling him into the woods? Did she say the word *fishing*? A wild thrumming started inside William's body. Then he thought, You wanted an adventure—here it is! He forced himself to look up, through the buzz and noise of his fear. He saw vast green trees, sharp against the blue. He saw white clouds sailing overhead and the darker shapes of a great pine, with a bright red bird hiding in the shadows. Then fear wrapped around him again, blocking out all sights for a moment.

When she reached the stream, Rose found a dry rock to sit on. Taking William out of her pocket, she propped him against a stone. His hair stood up wildly around his head. She wasn't sure, but his cheeks seemed pale and his mouth tight.

"William," she said softly, "we're going fishing. Don't worry."

He sighed. Rose did not notice. He saw water rushing past his toes, beautiful, clear water. Rose tied the end of her fishing twine around a piece of cheese and did the same with William's. Then she propped the tiny pole in William's hands and whispered, "I'll help you if you get a bite." Nervously she looked over her shoulder. She hoped no one could hear or see her talking to a doll.

Rose dropped her line into the stream and watched the silver water leaping over the pebbly bottom. The trees blew overhead, now letting sun splash the surface, now darkening the water. A frog peered at her from a nearby rock.

Gripping the rod as best he could, William stopped being quite so afraid. Rose wasn't going to hurt him or leave him in the woods. He was fishing in a real stream, just as he had wished! Somehow, in spite of her pink face and the dent in her chin, this girl had heard his wish and answered it. William let out a long sigh. The water gleamed in his eyes, sun shone down on his head, and he was suddenly so happy he thought he might fly off into the sky.

Then something tugged on his line. *"Rose!"* he yelled, but she did not hear. She was busy pulling on her line, shouting out, "Fish!" and flailing about with her arms. In the confusion and noise, she did not notice William, did not see that his hands were tangled in the fish line and he was sliding into the water.

"Rose!" he called again, loudly, despairingly. Water closed over his head, and he saw the fat, green shape of a frog holding the other end of his line. It was even chewing the piece of cheese, he saw, gulping it down greedily and sending up little bubbles to the surface.

The frog kept tugging on the line, pulling William

deeper and deeper into the pool where the stream bubbled and foamed from a small waterfall. One last, great tug from the frog freed William's hands from the line. Lying on the bottom of the stream, he saw some strange water creature dragging a mass of pebbles behind it. He saw something that looked like a huge white spider scuttle under a rock. Then there was a nibble on his left foot and he shouted. It was a tiny silver fish, the one he wanted for Mama. Reaching out for the fish, he snagged his thumb in its gills. "Got you!" he burbled.

Then fingers closed around William and he shot into sunlight and air.

"Oh, William, I'm sorry! Are you all right?" Rose brought him up to her eyes. "I was so excited about my fish that I didn't notice..." She stopped and sucked in a breath.

William shouted, *"I caught my first fish, Rose!"* It flopped against him, thrashing back and forth. Just then he loved Rose, even her carelessness that had let him slide into the water without her seeing.

"A tiny silver fish," she whispered. "And you caught it by yourself. That's what you wanted."

Rose began to shiver. If she hadn't been so afraid of what Emily would say, she might have dropped William and run off through the woods. Instead she wrapped him in her not very clean handkerchief and tucked him into her pocket, along with the fish. By now it had stopped flopping against William's wrist.

Quiet and subdued, Rose crept up to the dollhouse and was relieved to see that Emily was elsewhere. It was one thing to imagine that a doll wanted things; it was another to have that wish actually come true. How could she explain the fish to Emily? How could she explain it to herself? Her head felt cottony and hot, as if she had a fever. The words *dolls, fish,* and *wishes* bounced about in her brain as she set the fish aside.

Stripping off William's wet clothes, Rose put him in his old gray pants and faded shirt. They were ugly, but at least they were clean and dry. And the blue shirt, while slightly ripped, would do. His chest seemed oddly bare to Rose as she fastened the tiny buttons, setting him in a chair by the kitchen table. She arranged all the other dolls in the kitchen, thinking, They will want to see the fish, too.

"William! You're all right!" Hettie exclaimed.

"You're back, safe and sound. Did she hurt you?" Papa asked with a worried frown.

"I'm not hurt at all, and look, everyone—I caught a fish!" crowed William.

"A fish, a real one, silver and shiny. How fresh it smells!" Hettie cried as Rose stood her next to the stove.

"Oh, won't we have a feast tonight! I haven't had fish in I don't know how many years—if ever," Papa said doubtfully.

Violet wrinkled her nose at the creature. It looked messy and disturbing, altogether too alive for her tastes. She preferred tea and the small bits of buttered toast that Emily put down for them to eat.

"What a clever boy," said Hettie. "How ever did you catch it?"

William said, "I went for an adventure underwater and saw a fat frog. And I caught this on the end of my thumb! I think Rose is a nice girl now, not mean at all." He smiled at her, but she did not see.

Shivering, she put the fish in a pan beside Hettie. "Have a good supper," Rose whispered, and ran from the dollhouse.

chapter 12

WHEN THE SUN rose the next morning, rays slanted across the kitchen table of the dollhouse. The fish on the stove had a somewhat floppy look. The family around the table was disappointed that Rose had not cooked the fish, but it was what they had expected. People just didn't think.

"We must try harder to get Walter back today," sighed Papa. "Fish are all very well, but where is our baby? Your mama and I did hear him murmur."

"So did I," said William, "and I thought I heard him say 'tree.'"

Violet kept quiet. Why was *she* the only one not to hear darling Walter?

"We know he's somewhere not too far away, because our thoughts can only travel a little way," Papa went on. "But we don't know *where*. And we don't know *how* to get to him."

"Too bad we don't still have a boy in the house," William said. "Remember, one of Alice's brothers had a motorcar? We could have gone for a drive in it and found Walter."

"Mmmm," considered Papa. "Then we've got to come up with something else. Think, dear ones, think!" he commanded.

William put his head in his hands; small thoughts like balls bounced about inside. *Car, horse, person.*

Violet said sharply, "Pooh! I can do that, too!" She cupped her head in her hands, but all she could think of was that horrible fish and its staring eye.

Hettie had ideas bounding about inside her head, too, but they were memories of Walter: what he had looked like when he was first made; his first words; his first song.

Papa suddenly sat up straighter. "Didn't Alice's family used to have a creature? Remember, Hettie?"

"Not that little thing like a mouse that ran around inside a cage." Hettie looked disgusted.

"No, not that," Papa exclaimed. "The other thing— with fur!"

"Dog!" William shouted. "They had a dog! It tried to lick us once, remember? And it tried to chew Walter, but the porcelain hurt its teeth."

"Hush, William!" cried Hettie from the stove.

"But what good is a dog?" Violet said. "How could it help us find Walter?"

"We could snag our fingers in its fur, Violet, and go for rides on it...out past the grass to where the trees grow. We could find Walter...and bring him back," William said slowly, puzzling it out as he spoke.

"Yes, yes!" Papa said excitedly. "That's it! A dog is a horse for dolls, William! But how will we tell the girls?"

"Don't you worry about that," William said confidently. "I will speak to Rose. She can hear me now."

"A dog?" Mother said at the breakfast table. "Why would you want a dog, Rose?"

"I don't know. It just came into my head. Not a big dog, Mother—something nice and furry with not too many teeth. Something cozy that might like to curl up on our beds at night."

Startled, Emily raised her head and smiled at Rose. "What a great idea!"

What put the thought in her head? Rose wondered. She'd been sitting here, chewing on some granola, when the words just spun into her brain. *Dog. Get a dog.* She was surprised at first, but then she thought how the dog could comfort her at night in her bedroom full of scary sounds.

"Yes, something to keep me company at night," Rose said, not wanting to admit how she slept with the covers pulled tight over her head.

Mother frowned. "But that would be something else

for you and Emily to fight over. You'd have to share and take turns."

"We would, we would!" Emily said eagerly. "We're getting better, didn't you notice? Yesterday we got through a whole day without arguing. We're trying, Mother!"

Mother nibbled her toast, swallowed, then smiled reluctantly. "It isn't just up to me. Gran has to agree, because this is her house, and so does Daddy. But I remember reading that people with pets are healthier."

"Dad could take it for walks every day, Mother. Wouldn't that be a good thing?" asked Rose, clasping her hands tightly together under the table.

Mother paused for a moment and then said, "I guess it would. And maybe a dog would make this house seem more like a home."

"It would!" Emily exclaimed. "We couldn't have a dog in the city because there was no place to keep one, remember?"

"The landlord wouldn't let us have one anyway," Mother said. "I like this idea. Let's talk about it again at lunchtime."

"A dog?" Gran said, setting soup bowls on the table. "I don't know, girls. I haven't had one in this house since my children were little."

"Flossie!" Dad exclaimed. "We had her when I was ten years old. She was a great dog, except she kept trying to herd the children in the neighborhood."

"Well, that's because she was a sheepdog," said Gran. "We could get something a bit smaller." She caught herself and laughed. "I'm already talking as if it's decided, aren't I? What do you think, Henry?"

"I'd like a dog," Dad said slowly. "All those years in the city we could never have animals. Now we can do things differently. A dog could bring me my paper and slippers."

Emily looked at Rose and Rose looked back. It was going to work, if only nothing went wrong....

"What kind?" Emily said, jiggling her leg. "What kind should we get, I mean?"

"Let's go to the pound," Mother said. "That way we can get an animal that someone abandoned."

"But it has to be nice!" Emily said. "Not one that bites or..."

"Chews on dolls," Gran said.

Emily stared at her, horrified. "A dog wouldn't do that, would it?"

"Ours did, a long time ago," Gran mused. "In fact, I think it chewed on the very doll that you're looking for, Emily. The littlest one."

"Did he get hurt?" Emily asked anxiously.

"No, because he's made of porcelain—the only one that's all porcelain." Gran smiled.

When the table was cleared and the dishes put away, the whole family climbed into the car and set off for the pound. It turned out to be in someone's backyard, with dogs side by side in fenced-in sections. As Emily and Rose walked by the pens, the dogs leaped up on the fence and barked, wagging their tails furiously.

"Look!" Rose crouched down by one pen. "I like this black furry one." *Lots of hair*—the words came unbidden into her mind.

"Mmm." Mother took Rose's hand and helped her up. "Looks like a terrier, honey. They tend to dig in the sofa."

"And hard to train," said Dad. Whistling, he strode around looking at the dogs.

Emily could hardly bear it. Mouths wide and panting, the dogs waited so eagerly. Each needed a home, but they could only rescue one animal.

"How can people do it?" Emily exclaimed. "Leave a dog all on its own." She twisted her hands together.

The woman who ran the pound smiled at her. "You'd be surprised at what people do. Sometimes they just dump the animal out of the car or move and don't take the dog with them."

"Oh," sighed Rose.

Dad stopped whistling as he came to another pen. "I like this Lab."

Rose stared at the short-haired dog. "Not enough fur, Dad."

"Why does it have to be furry?" Emily grabbed her sister's arm.

Rose gave her a strange look. "I'm not sure—it just does."

"How about this, girls?" Mother stopped in front of a compact dog with thick, curly brown hair. "It looks like it's got some poodle in it, and they're very smart dogs."

The woman nodded. "Hannah's lovely, about two years old, so you don't have to go through the puppy stage, and she probably won't shed very much."

Wagging her long, feathery tail, the dog stared at them with warm brown eyes.

Emily squeezed her sister's arm. "This one, Rose. She's got lots of fur, and I like the name Hannah."

"Sit, Hannah; down, Hannah," Dad tried out the commands. The dog pricked her ears and sat.

"Yes, she's just right," Gran agreed.

"Can I have her tonight," Rose whispered, "if you get her tomorrow?"

"All right." Emily nodded.

"Do you have a blanket to put under her?" asked the woman. "For the ride home?"

Mother shook her head. "We didn't think of it."

"She'll be all right," Rose said confidently. "You can tell Hannah won't throw up."

"You hope." Dad picked up the dog as the woman opened the fence. Hannah squirmed happily in his arms and jumped into the back of the car.

"I think she's ridden in a station wagon before," the woman said, closing the back door.

"Good-bye, thank you!" they chorused, and drove off with Hannah waving her tail.

"I can't believe it!" Mother exclaimed. "Careful us, always planning. We got a dog just like that!" She snapped her fingers.

As the car headed out onto the main road, Dad said, "We're going to do *more* things just like that, out of the blue. I'm tired of planning. I'm tired of being careful, Marge."

Emily gave Rose a glance, and Rose looked back at her. But, thought Rose, this wasn't out of the blue at all. It was meant to be.

chapter 13

J UST WAIT,'' Emily whispered to the dog be-
hind them, "wait till you meet Violet and William and
Papa and Hettie. Maybe you'll be able to hear them.
Maybe you can help us find Walter."

The dog stretched out and licked Emily's cheek.
"Oooh! I got a dog kiss!"

Rose held her cheek close to the dog. "I want one,
too."

As if she knew that Rose wouldn't like a real lick,
Hannah just touched her nose to Rose's skin.

"*That* is a very intelligent dog," Gran said as they turned into their driveway and parked.

When they opened the wagon door, Hannah jumped down and walked up and down in front of the house, sniffing everything and peeing behind the sunflowers. Then she trotted up the front steps and into the kitchen.

"Come on!" Rose said, running ahead of the dog. "Come upstairs, Hannah." The dog ran after her, with Emily close behind. When they stopped by the dollhouse, Hannah sat on her haunches and gave a sharp yap.

"What's that!" Papa yelled, startled awake from his doze at the kitchen table. His tea spilled and dripped off the table.

"A monster!" Violet shrieked.

"A bison," Hettie shouted. "It's a bison. Look at its fur!"

"A dog," said William calmly, "just what I wished for. A nice furry dog with lots of hair for us to hold on to."

"Why would we want to hold on to a bison's fur?" Hettie moaned.

"A dog's fur, Mama," William corrected her. "Because it is going to take us to Walter and bring Walter home." He leaned back in his chair, smiling slightly. He felt as if he had won a race.

"Why did Hannah bark?" Rose asked, crouching by the dollhouse.

Emily smiled. "I think she's saying hello."

The dog lay down and sniffed the dollhouse kitchen. Her nose quivered. Suddenly Rose remembered the fish.

She wasn't ready to tell Emily about it; it was *her* adventure with *her* doll, something not even Emily, with her dream of the dolls, could do. So she got up quickly, tugged on the dog's collar, and said, "Come with me. Come see *my* room." Hannah followed at her heels and jumped easily onto Rose's bed. The dog circled once, twice, and lay down with a sigh.

"See? She likes my room; she likes it!" Rose crowed.

"You can tell Hannah wants to be here tonight." Emily gazed sadly at the dog. But Hannah settled her nose cozily between her paws, sighed, and fell into a deep sleep.

"She hasn't been in a home for a while," said Gran from the doorway. "Hannah's got a lot to get used to. Just leave her be for a while. Come downstairs and have a snack."

As Gran and the girls walked past the dollhouse, Violet said to William, "That's a dog?" Her ears hurt from the creature's shout. "That is going to *help* us?"

"Yes," said William. "You watch. That dog will be our salvation."

"Salvation, pooh! What do you know about salvation?" snapped Violet. She wasn't even sure what that meant.

William sat there with a wise smile on his face, which infuriated Violet. Then he said, "I know some things about salvation. I know that bringing Walter home will be Mama's salvation. I think that putting Walter on your lap will be yours. I know Papa will rest easy in his heart once our family is all together again."

"And what about you?" Violet asked grumpily.

"I have to find a heart," William said so softly that Violet only heard the word *heart*.

"Heart," she repeated, wishing she could pat her chest. Violet was sick of William and his certainties. She was tired of cold food badly prepared. She wished she had a red dress that would express how wild and daring she felt inside. And she wanted Walter on her lap again, to cuddle and sing songs to. She didn't think this dog was a good idea at all. Disaster loomed ahead of her, as tall and as solid as a tree in sunlight.

chapter 14

THE DOG had eaten a large supper of dog nuggets and lapped a bowl of water. The girls had bathed and had *Five Children and It* read to them on Rose's bed, with Hannah looking on and nudging the book out of Gran's lap.

"See, she likes the Psammead," Emily said. "Hannah likes magic things."

"I think we should close the door to your room, dear," Gran said, shutting the book. "We don't know if she's going to wander or what."

"No, no!" Rose sat bolt upright. "I can't stand to have

the door closed. And leave the light on in the hallway."

"All right, Rose. We'll have to trust that this dog knows about houses. She certainly *seems* to. Every time she's had to go out, she's used the animal door," Gran said, smiling. "I guess Hannah will be OK. Good night, girls." She saw Emily back to her room and waved.

"I still don't see how that monster is going to help us," Hettie said by the stove.

The hall light created eerie patches of darkness and light in the dollhouse. "I wish those girls would move us into the living room. I'm getting awfully tired of this kitchen," she complained. "I hope they don't play with that monster so much that they forget *us*!"

"That 'monster,' as you call him, Mama, is our wheels, our car, our electric train," said William.

"*Quoi?*" asked Violet, proud of remembering the French word for *what*.

"William means that we have no way to travel on our own," said Papa. "We can move a little but not enough to walk out to the forest to rescue Walter. And we might have to carry him home."

No one put into words what they were all thinking: that Walter could be a broken heap of legs and arms, impossible to gather up and bring back.

"And how are we going to drive the dog to the forest?" asked Violet sharply.

"We won't *drive* it, dear sister," William snapped; "we will *ride* it."

"Ride it?" Papa said, sitting straighter at the table. "How? Dogs don't have saddles, you know."

"Well, I thought we could grab on to the dog's fur—that's why it was important to get a dog with lots of hair—and hang on while it walks out to the forest," William explained.

"But what if it won't go to the woods?" asked Violet. "It might wander down the road to that strange place Rose left me in. That dog could go anywhere!"

"Well, if we can put our wishes into people's minds, why not into a dog's mind?" said William in a reasonable I-refuse-to-get-mad voice.

"But dogs don't use words!" exclaimed Violet. "At least humans, as stupid as they are, use words."

"You don't know that," said William, "because we've never tried it with an animal before. Let's try, right now."

"All right," challenged Violet, "go ahead."

William put his head into his hands, resting his elbows on the kitchen table. He imagined the dog in his mind and then pictured the dollhouse. He thought, Dogs can see, can't they? If I give her some pictures, maybe she'll do what I want. Then he sent out a picture of the fish on the table.

"See?" Violet said after they had waited for a while. "So much for your grand idea, William. I don't see any dog."

"Or bison," murmured Hettie, relieved that the huge shaggy beast had not appeared.

Papa raised his head. "What's that?" They listened and heard something clicking on the floorboards.

"Quick, Mama, cover the fish with a cloth. We don't want to give it to her just yet," William said.

"The monster!" Hettie exclaimed, as Hannah padded toward the dollhouse and sat in front of it. The dog wagged her tail slightly, stirring up the dust from the floor, and Hettie sneezed. The cloth covering the fish fluttered.

William spoke, "Nice doggy, good doggy. Take us for a ride and you can have a tasty treat." He imagined the dog lying down, and Hannah did so.

"Now," said Papa, taking charge. "William and I will ride the dog this time. No, not you, Violet," he said as she objected. "You were right when you said we don't know where this dog will go. William," he commanded, "you first."

Slowly William pushed himself away from the table. Pressing down with his hands, in a series of sharp jerks, he managed to almost stand upright. With locked knees he walked stiffly to the end of the kitchen counter. "Now, no falling down," he said to himself, "no tripping over the edge here." He steadied himself against the wall and put one foot out over the ledge at the end of their house. Suddenly he fell to the hallway floor and groaned. The dog nosed him gently, turning him over onto his back. She nosed him again, pressing him against the dollhouse wall until he slid upright.

"See," William said in a breathless voice. "She knows how to help. Good doggy, nice doggy." Reaching out, William thrust his hands into the dog's fur until they caught in the curls. He didn't feel very secure. He watched Papa walk carefully and slowly to the ledge and then half sit, half slide to the floor.

"You didn't fall!" he said.

"My legs are longer, William," said Papa with a proud smile.

"Put your hands right into the fur, Papa."

Arthur hesitated a moment, appeared to be talking to himself, and then stuck his hands deep into Hannah's coat. "This will be an adventure, William."

"All right, Papa?"

"All right, son."

Let's go! William pictured the dog rising and going through the hall, down the steps, and out the front door. To his great surprise and delight, William felt the dog rise, trot along the hall, and start down the steps.

"Ouch, ooh!" jerked out of Papa as he swung from side to side.

"Help!" yelled William as he fell off and bounced down the stairs to the bottom. It was dark as the bottom of a well there, and there were no sounds from the other rooms.

"Oh, my dear boy, are you all right?" called Papa. The dog stopped by the last step, with Papa still swinging against her fur.

William said, "It's a good thing we're mostly made out of wood, Papa. I'm all right." He sent an image of the dog lying beside him, and soon she did so. William stumbled forward and plunged his hands into her dense fur again. He pictured the dog standing and going outside.

The dog stood, trotted to the front entrance, and whined. In the murky gloom, William saw that the big oak door was tightly shut.

"Drat!" William said. "I forgot about these things. What should we do now, Papa?"

Arthur was near the dog's collar. Every time the dog moved, he thumped sickeningly against her side. But this was an adventure, the first he'd been on in many a year, and he was going to see it through.

"Tell it to go to the kitchen, William. Maybe there's a door there. I hope," he added in a whisper.

William pictured the kitchen and sent Hannah toward it.

"I'm tired of being jounced about, Papa," William complained. "I hope Walter appreciates this when we find him."

"*If* we find him," Papa added grimly. When the dog stopped, Papa saw there was a small door cut into the bottom of the big one.

"Hurray!" cried Papa. "I was right. Tell her to go through the little door, William."

William sent out a picture of the dog nosing the flap, and she did just that, pausing on the top step. "Oh! I forgot about stars, Papa. Look!"

The dark sky was scattered with gleaming points of light. A soft wind blew in their faces. Raising her head, Hannah sniffed the air deeply, thoroughly. She gave a happy sigh and bounded down the front steps.

"Now," Papa's words jerked out, "make her go to the woods, William."

"I'm trying," replied William in a muffled voice. His head had gotten stuck in the dog's fur, and he could not see. He tried picturing the woods, tall trees against the night sky. But the dog did not turn toward the woods. Suddenly she arched her back and raced to the meadow. Something jumped in front of her—a rabbit?—and she ran after it.

Grimly William hung on as he was flung backward and forward. He heard Papa give a small cry and wondered if he'd fallen off. How would he ever get Papa home again if he was dropped in the meadow? For a moment his head swung free of the fur and he looked out fearfully. Night rushed by. Stars poured overhead. The wind blew in his face as they galloped along. But if he was ever to deserve a heart, he would have to be brave. Then, just as suddenly as she had begun, the dog stopped.

"Papa? Are you all right?" he called. He heard a groan.

"William? Are you there? I don't know how much longer I can hold on!"

"It's all right, Papa. We'll go home. It's too dangerous."

"No, William, we must keep looking!"

"Papa, I'm afraid we might fall off and never get back again." He formed an image of the house, and the dog turned and loped back to the kitchen steps. Up one, they jolted alarmingly. Up two, William almost fell off.

Papa said, "Tell her to go through."

"All right," William answered, his nose stuck in the dog's fur. But before he could send an image, the dog squeezed through the opening. Then she trotted to the staircase, bounded up, and stopped in front of the dollhouse.

"William!" Hettie called. "Are you all right? Is Arthur there, too?"

Papa clattered to the hallway floor as William unclenched his stiff fingers and slid off the dog.

"Mama?" he called. "Can you toss that fish onto the floor?"

"I'll try," Hettie replied. Stiffly she pushed at the fish and it fell off the stove.

An eager, wet black nose was thrust into the kitchen. "Eeek!" shrieked Hettie. "The bison will eat us!"

The dog whuffed, blowing Hettie onto the floor. She was speechless with fear. All she could see was a mouth full of white, gleaming teeth and a blood red tongue searching, licking. Suddenly it lapped up the fish, and the dog withdrew.

"Oh my!" whimpered Hettie, "oh my."

"Mama, it's all right. The dog would never hurt you." I think, he said to himself as the dog trotted down the hallway and went back to Rose's room.

"Did you find Walter?" Hettie whispered. "Did you get to the woods?"

"No," answered William. "Sorry, Mama, but the dog wouldn't go to the woods, and we almost fell off. It was too dangerous."

"That's all right," Hettie sighed. "You did the best you could. But what will the girls think when they see us in these different positions tomorrow? We're all on the floor except Violet."

"What an adventure!" Papa exclaimed. "I'm too tired

to walk into our house tonight. I think I'll sleep right here."

William sighed in agreement. His legs and arms felt loose from the jolting ride and the fall. His head swam with pictures, smells, and fear. Wishing he could close his eyes, he finally slept.

chapter 15

WHEN ROSE opened her eyes the next morn-
ing, it was to see their dog lying asleep on the foot of her
bed. She wiggled her toes under Hannah's warmth and
sighed happily. Knowing that Hannah would wake up if
anything tried to come into her room, Rose had slept
soundly and deeply.

Humming to herself, Rose dressed and went out into
the hallway, with the dog pattering behind. Emily was
already crouched in front of the dollhouse.

"Rose? Did you look at them this morning?"

"Not yet." Rose knelt beside her. "Did you put William and Papa on the floor?"

"Of course not!" Emily picked Hettie off the blue-and-white tiles of the kitchen and settled her at the table. "Do you think the dog got into the dollhouse?"

Hannah lay on the floor, swishing her tail.

Quickly Rose looked to see if the fish was still there, but it had gone. Maybe the dog ate it last night and scattered the dolls about. Could she tell Emily about it?

"It's such a mystery." Emily sighed. "I don't know. If we can't find Walter, we can just give up the idea of their ever being happy."

"Well, there's one mystery I can solve," Rose said, finally deciding. "Two days ago—you remember when I didn't have lunch?"

"Yup, I remember."

"I took William in my pocket out to the stream."

"Rose!" Emily knelt back on her heels and stared at her sister. "Why did you do that? Not to be..."

"No, not to be mean," Rose interrupted. "It's hard to explain. I was thinking about Violet and how she hated that dress. And that made me wonder if dolls *did* have feelings—sort of. Anyway," she rushed on, "I thought William might want to go fishing." She stopped for a moment, remembering the words that had sparked in her brain, clear and sharp as stars.

Her sister just looked at her.

"So, we went fishing out back in the woods," Rose said.

"Did you catch anything?"

"Yes! William did—a little silver fish, on his thumb." She was not going to tell Emily how she'd forgotten about William and let him slide into the stream. "And I brought it back and put it on the doll's stove."

"Raw?"

"Well, I couldn't cook it, could I? Then I'd have to *explain* to everyone downstairs what happened."

"OK, I see. So maybe Hannah ate the fish, is that what you think?"

"Yes. And she probably scattered the dolls onto the floor at the same time."

"No, no, oh, deary me, no," said Hettie. "They've got it *all* wrong. How can they be so stupid? They're so big, you'd think they'd be smarter, Arthur."

"Well, they're not dolls, are they?" said Papa. "They don't think as we do."

Emily grinned a wide, curving smile, and hugged her sister fiercely. "You can hear the dolls now!" Emily wanted to shout, "You see? They do have feelings; they do want things!"

"Yeah!" Rose said in a surprised voice. "I guess I can." Then louder, "I guess I can!"

Humming busily, Rose picked up Papa and dusted him off. "Time to go back in the house, Papa. You're a little wet."

"Probably from the dog's tongue," she added.

"But so's William," Emily said, as she picked the boy doll up and straightened his blue shirt. "And the paint's chipped a bit on his elbow."

"Look." Rose held out Papa. "Look at his hands."

In Papa's right hand were some brown curly hairs.

"Uh, oh," muttered Papa, "now we're in for it. They'll start putting two and two together, locking up the dog at night, who knows what else! Then we will be stuck."

William answered from Emily's hand, "Don't worry—they're on our side, remember? We don't have to keep secrets from them."

"Of course we do. Dolls always have secrets from humans!" Papa answered, wishing Rose would put him down. His arms and hands ached from last night, and he felt soiled and mussed from his race through the grass. "I wish I could have a bath," he murmured.

"I wonder what it means. It's a mystery," Emily sighed. "The whole thing is a mystery," she repeated.

Rose patted her sister awkwardly on the shoulder. "We'll figure it out, Emily, don't worry," she said, surprising herself and her sister.

"I think it's high time someone sent them a message," Papa said, as Rose settled him on the couch. "We've got to enlist their help."

"What does *that* mean?" Violet said fretfully.

"It means we've got to get the people to help us look for Walter," said Hettie.

"And how do we do that?" Violet asked.

"Talk to the girls," William answered, still in Emily's hand. "Remember that time we called to Walter? He only made a little sound and then said 'tree.'"

"Who's going to give the girls a picture?" asked Papa.

"I am," William declared. "Rose can hear me now. She's my friend." Concentrating all of his will on the large face near him, William thought: *Woods, Rose, Walter is in the woods. The woods.* And then he pictured tall green trees towering overhead.

Rose's eyes widened and she backed away from the dollhouse.

"What? What is it?" Emily said nervously, her fingers tightening on William.

"He's...he's..." Rose pointed at the boy doll.

"Talking to you?" Emily finished for her.

Rose just nodded.

"So what does he *say*?"

"Trees, Emily. The woods."

Emily jumped up. "Then that's where we're going right now to look for Walter!" She picked up Papa doll in her other hand.

Rose thought the shivery feeling she had inside might be helped by breakfast. "Not till after we eat!" she said, looking at the two dolls in Emily's hands. Did they look excited, expectant somehow? She wasn't sure.

"All right, all right! Though how you can choose food over adventure!" Emily started down the hall. Sighing, Rose followed, with the dog trotting beside.

I don't like this, these voices in my mind, she thought. But she wanted to find Walter, too. What was it her sister said? If they made a home for the dolls, then that would help make a home for their family, too.

chapter 16

IN THE KITCHEN Gran was chopping apples while Mother peeled, carefully curling the long, red skin off the white flesh. Then Gran beat the apples into a bowl full of batter.

"Apple pancakes?" Rose came and stood beside her mother.

"Yup, your favorite, if I remember." Mother gave Rose a spoon to lick.

"Oh, yes!" Rose clattered onto a chair at the kitchen table, while Emily sat beside her.

"Where's Dad?" Emily asked, fiddling with her fork.

"Oh, I know. I bet he's out taking his consti...consti...What do you call it?"

"His constitutional," Gran finished, laughing. With deft movements she ladled batter onto the hot griddle.

"We're going on a constitutional after breakfast," Rose said happily. "With our..." She stopped herself just in time. She wasn't going to talk about the dolls with Mother or Gran, not like Emily, even if she *did* hear tiny voices in her mind.

"Good idea." Gran put full plates in front of the girls. "And it's a lovely day outside, bright and sunny."

After breakfast Emily pulled her knapsack out of the closet and put William and Papa inside.

"Wait," Rose said, as her sister started for the door. "Let's make some snacks. Who knows how long we'll be out in the woods?"

"The woods, girls?" Gran asked. "Wait a minute." She began to rummage in a drawer under the wall stove. "It used to be here...ah!" She drew out a whistle on a string and put it around Rose's neck. "If my kids ever got lost in the woods, they'd blow this and we'd hear them. You'd better wear this, then."

"All right." Rose frowned as she thought of getting lost in the woods, wandering helplessly among the trees until darkness came. Living in the city did not prepare you for life in the woods, she wanted to shout, but she didn't.

Emily slapped some peanut butter on Ritz crackers and stuck them together, enough to make twelve small sandwiches. Mother handed her two oranges and two bottles of Orangina.

"Thanks, Mother." Emily stuffed the food into her knapsack, being careful to keep the dolls on top.

"Oof!" Papa said. "What are these things?"

"Food, Papa," replied William, lying on Ritz crackers. "Doesn't it smell delicious?"

"My," sighed Papa. "All this food for two girls, and they've just eaten breakfast. No wonder they're so huge!"

"Once we're in the woods, Papa—I *hope* we're right in thinking Walter's in the woods; he did only say 'tree'—we can call to him."

As Emily headed for the door, Mother cautioned, "Be back by lunch, Rose and Emily. Then we won't worry."

"OK, but don't worry about us. We'll be fine. William will tell us where to go," said Emily.

Mother gave her a puzzled look, then kissed her soundly. "Bye."

Emily pushed open the screen door, and out they went, the dog trotting beside. They went through the meadow, where tall grasses brushed their knees and black-eyed Susans nodded in the wind. Birds swooped overhead.

"Barn swallows." Emily pointed. "Gran told me they leave at the end of August, just before school starts."

"Don't say that word!"

"But we have to, Rose. It's going to happen, even if we don't want it to. I'll be in third grade and . . ."

"I know what I'll be!" Fourth grade. New people. Staring eyes. Walking by kids who won't even say hello, she thought.

Soon they were at the entrance to the woods, where great swags of bittersweet hung from dark pines. Pushing past the branches, Emily stepped on a carpet of shiny green leaves.

Rose sighed. It was beautiful in the woods, the air quiet and still. School seemed far away, something that might happen to another girl, not her. "Where do we start?" she asked.

"I guess anyplace, Rose." Emily picked up a stick and began to swat at low branches. She wasn't sure just what she was looking for. The dog walked ahead, nose to the ground, tail waving.

Inside the knapsack William asked, "Have they found anything yet?" He tried to move but was stuck facedown with his head on a cracker.

"I don't think so. Shouldn't we call to Walter? Maybe he's nearby and can give us some clues," Papa said.

"All right. Together now, like before." *Walter, where are you? We are here in the woods. Talk to us.* Their words, uttered in a tone far too high for humans to hear, fanned out through the air, stopping the dog as she nosed last year's leaves.

When the dog raised her head, listening, Emily asked, "What is it, Hannah? Did you hear something?" She crouched beside the dog, petting her thick, warm coat.

Then Hannah lowered her head to the ground again, nuzzling some moss. The girls continued to poke through the leaves and pine needles covering the ground, upturning rocks and letting out little cries as they discovered newts and small gray frogs. Hannah jumped after one of the frogs, barking excitedly until it disappeared in a stone wall.

"Maybe Walter heard the dog barking," said Papa. "Let's try again." *Walter, where are you? Talk to us!*

This time it was not a murmur that came back to them. It was words, real words, clear and strong. *Come find me. I am near. And lonely.*

A picture of a dark tunnel came with the words. "Did you get that, Papa? The words? And the picture?" William shouted.

"Yes, yes! He is nearby, in something dark...and round," Papa exclaimed.

William thought for a while and then cried, "I know, I know! Alice read a story once about another little girl called Alice who fell down a rabbit hole. Maybe it's a rabbit hole—dark and round, just like the story."

"My smart boy," Papa said proudly.

"Rose?" Emily sighed and sat down on a mossy stone. "I don't know how we're ever going to find Walter. He could be *anywhere* out here."

"Mmmm," said Rose. Something was tapping inside...something to do with a circle... Suddenly she closed her mind. She didn't *want* someone else's thoughts in her mind. It was frightening, like a secret door opening to let in spidery creatures.

Quickly she turned and headed out of the woods.

"Where're you going, Rose?" called Emily, hurrying after her. "We can't give up so soon!"

"Who's giving up?" Rose swatted her stick at the

bittersweet overhead. "I'm just tired of looking, that's all."

"But this is our first try. We should . . ."

"I'm tired!" Rose didn't even turn around.

"Scared is more like it," William said from inside the pack. "I think I frightened her, Papa, putting things in her mind. This time she wouldn't listen."

"Well," said Papa, "she's only a girl, after all. Give her time. We'll try again another day. But, oh, to be so close!"

"We'll try again another day," echoed Emily. She followed her sister out of the woods into the brilliant sunlight, wondering why Rose had suddenly stopped looking.

chapter 17

HETTIE SAT at the kitchen table, hands clasped
before her. She had broken a cardinal rule—never ever
change positions after a child sets you down. She hadn't
had her hands clasped when Emily and Rose left with
William and Arthur, but she was so worried she had to
do something.

Violet knocked her elbow against the table. "Mama, I
have to move! We've been in this kitchen for *years!*"

"I know, dear, I know," Hettie soothed. "But you
mustn't. It's bad enough I've got my hands on the table,

and you've moved, too, I see. I wish..." Hettie just *knew* something was wrong. Walter was falling to pieces in a dark hole somewhere, and when they found him, *if* they found him, he would be a bundle of rags and broken bits of porcelain. She moaned.

"Mama!" Violet said. Jerkily she reached out and patted Hettie. "Mama, please stop worrying. I'm sure Papa and William are all right. They were in Emily's sack, so they cannot get lost or left behind."

"How do you know?" Mama said sharply. "Anything can happen with children and dogs. A doll is little, of no account. He can be lost, left behind, fall under a bush or down a hole. That bison could carry William off in his mouth."

"*Her* mouth," corrected Violet. "William says it's a her."

"Her mouth, his mouth, what's the difference when you're lost!" Hettie snapped. "It's too dangerous, all this gallivanting about. Anything can happen!" she repeated in a dismal tone. "Sometimes I almost wish..." She paused and sighed.

"Wish what, Mama?" Violet prompted.

"I almost wish the children had left us in the dark. Yes, I do! Then I had no worries, no sorrow, just a dark blanket of sleep around me. It was safe and warm, and I didn't know that..." She gulped. "I didn't know that Walter was lost."

"Mama," Violet said gently. She wanted to get up and hug her but was afraid to do so. They had already broken the rules, though she doubted the girls would notice. They were too busy with that beast now to notice anything.

"Mama, the dark time is over. We can't go back to it, even if we wished it. As long as they play with us, we are alive." Violet started at the sound of footsteps outside. Would the girls see that Mama had her hands on the kitchen table?

"We're back!" shouted Papa. Emily set him and William on the two chairs. With one quick movement, the girl picked up Violet and Hettie, placing them on the two chairs in the living room.

"Oh, it's good to be home, Hettie, dear!" said Papa.

"Did you, did you?" Hettie asked.

Papa shook his head. "No, we didn't find Walter, but we *heard* him quite clearly this time. He was near us in the big woods."

"Oh!" cried Hettie and Violet together.

"But the girls and the dog couldn't find the hole he's in," said William. "Rose wouldn't listen to me, though I tried to tell her."

"So near and yet so far," said Hettie.

"Do not despair, Mother," said William in a round tone. "Disappointment is our lot. Or is it that man is born to evil as the sparks fly upward?" He tested the words in his mouth.

"Stop it!" Violet snapped. "We don't need that kind of depressing talk. Born to evil, indeed. I, for one, am not born to evil." Violet smiled, thankful to be back in her new green dress. "*I* was born for beauty and flowers and romance."

"A lot of romance you're going to find in a dollhouse," teased William.

"Hush, children, hush. I can't think with you two arguing. Now, we know Walter is near; we are closing in on him, Hettie. We mustn't give up hope!" declared Papa.

"The darkest hour is before the dawn," intoned William.

Emily sat back on her heels, watching the dolls. There was an air of excitement rising from them, like golden fizzy sparks. She wished Rose had waited to get her snack until later and was here with her.

"I'm sorry we didn't find Walter," Emily whispered. "We tried. We'll try again." She stood and went back downstairs to rejoin her family.

"Tonight," said Papa. "We will try again tonight."

"Not with that beast, Arthur!" Hettie exclaimed.

"Of course with the dog," Papa said reassuringly. "She's a good animal, and William can make her do things."

"And this time I'm coming, too," declared Violet.

Darkness came slowly to the dollhouse, too slowly for Papa. Perched on the edge of the chair, he waited for the blackness that would cover their movements. First it was pink on the floor of the dollhouse. After what seemed an age, the pink faded to a light gray. Then bits of darkness caught in the corners like dust until the entire floor was black.

Papa heard the big girls settling down to sleep and Emily calling out that it was cozy having Hannah on her bed.

"How will we get the dog to come?" William asked. "We used up the fish. Emily gave us some bits of toast and jam. Do you think that will work?"

"Oh, don't give them to the dog, William!" Violet exclaimed. "They're for my breakfast—I mean our breakfast."

"Can't you just *call* the dog to come, William?" Papa asked, but William did not answer. Papa was dressed for the expedition tonight. He had found a paper clip on the floor in front of the dollhouse. When the girls were downstairs eating lunch, he had walked carefully toward it, bent over, and picked it up, saying, "You never know when you might need a tool." He did not say what was in his mind: that if Walter was in pieces, they would need something to hold him together before they could ride on the dog.

It was Hettie, in her practical way, who voiced their worries. "Arthur, dear, don't you think we should bring some rope with us? What if Walter is broken up? We'll need to tie him together before he can go on the bison."

"I know where there's some rope, Mama," William said. "Up in our attic. I remember seeing one of our old blankets there. I think if we rip some threads off it, that would do."

"Capital!" Papa exclaimed, hoping he sounded like a commanding officer in a British regiment. "Can you go upstairs and get it? Everyone's in bed now."

"Of course I can," William said stoutly. Yet he worried that his legs would not bend enough to go up the steep stairs to the attic. Those long years lying forgotten and asleep in the dark had made it so hard to move. But he was going to try; he *had* to try.

Carefully he eased himself upright by pressing down against the chair's arms. He rose and rocked on his heels.

"All right, my boy, all right. You're doing fine," Papa encouraged him.

"Now!" William said to himself, and put one foot forward, then another. He reached the stairs and began to climb. Swinging one foot onto the first step, he raised the other for the second step and heard a dull click.

"I'm stuck!" he cried. "My knees won't bend anymore!" He clutched the stair railings and hung on.

"Try, William, oh, try," cried Violet.

"Maybe if you take a deep breath, it will work," Papa said. If he had been human, he would have been a believer in cold showers, vigorous exercise before dawn, and staying away from the marsh air.

"No," said Hettie. "If his legs don't work now, they are not going to change. Come down from the stairs, William."

William took his hands off the stair railings and fell backward onto the hall floor. His head bounced once, twice, and then lay still. He saw stars and heard the faint chirping of birds.

"Ouch! My poor head."

"Oh, William, oh, dear," came a confused babble of voices.

After a moment William was able to raise himself onto his elbows and pull himself upright by the stair railings. "I'm all right—stop worrying," he said. "It's just my leg is sort of stuck out. I'll call that dog, and we will search for Walter—without the rope." He thought of the dog, then imagined her coming to them in the dollhouse. For good measure he called, *Come, dog, to the dollhouse. We need you.*

In a matter of seconds they heard paws clicking on floorboards. As the dog lay down in front of the dollhouse, she looked just like a brown rug, thought Violet. Only the dog's furry ears moved back and forth.

"Now," declared Hettie, "this time I am coming. I refuse to be left behind, waiting and worrying!"

"And I'm coming, too." Violet rose from the sofa and lurched forward. Raising her head, Hannah eyed the dolls uneasily as they walked jerkily toward her.

William had the presence of mind to grab a piece of jam-covered toast and hold it out to Hannah. She licked jam off his fingers delicately, sniffed him all over, and wagged her tail.

"See? She knows me; she's my friend."

"You hope," said Violet. "Where do I go?"

"Just find a clump of fur and hang on, Vi," said William.

"You know I hate that nickname," Violet complained, clutching a bunch of hair near the collar.

Hettie stepped forward and pushed her hands into the thick hair by the dog's tail. Papa hoisted himself up beside her, and William grabbed the fur at Hannah's middle.

"All right, everyone?" Papa asked, imagining himself at the head of a column of soliders, ready for battle.

"All right," they chorused, and William sent an image of the animal door into the dog's mind. Quickly Hannah rose, trotted along the hall, down the stairs, and into the kitchen.

"Oh, oh my . . ." came the confused cries of the dolls as they swung from side to side. William pictured a dog walking steadily and calmly, which slowed Hannah a little.

"Ah!" exclaimed William. "Here we are." Hannah pushed through the opening and stood on the steps.

"Stars!" Hettie exclaimed. "Oh, look."

Amid the delighted cries of the dolls, Hannah sniffed the night wind and wagged her tail. What she thought of four stiff, wooden figures bouncing against her body, none of the dolls ever knew, though they later wondered. William sent out an image of trees and a stone wall, and Hannah gave a short, happy bark, loping toward the woods.

"Are you all right?" gasped William.

"Yes," said Papa bravely.

"I . . . guess . . . so," Mama's words jerked out.

Violet did not answer; she was too busy hanging on.

"Don't let go—we're heading for the woods!" commanded Papa.

Overhead the stars strung themselves across the sky in a glittering banner. The wind blew in their faces, and Hettie's head swam. She had forgotten the night. Was everyone all right? Would she ever hold dear Walter close again?

chapter 18

FIELD GRASSES brushed the dolls as Hannah trotted along the path to the woods.

"Hold on!" Papa called.

"Don't despair!" yelled William.

Violet did not answer, nor did Hettie. Moonlight slipped across her, then disappeared like silver ribbons floating overhead. Then something black and immense blocked out the moon.

"What is that?" Hettie asked in a wavering voice.

"Trees, Mama," William replied. "Don't be frightened; we're in the woods."

Suddenly the dog began to race in circles, uttering short, sharp barks. Something ran ahead of them, and Hannah jumped at a near pine, scrabbling at the tree and barking furiously.

"Don't let go!" yelled William.

Papa tried to grip the dog's fur more tightly, but his fingers were stiff and sore. The fur slid between them, and he dropped to the ground as the dog leaped ahead. "Help!" he cried.

"Oooh!" said Hettie, slipping into a nest of wet, clammy mushrooms.

"Oh my," said William, sliding down onto a pile of damp leaves near the barking dog. A creature high in the branches gave a trill and then a long *chrrrrrrr!*

Violet disdained to say anything; *she* was used to being tossed about, exposed to dew and dampness, and spending nights out in the wilderness. I will show them how to go on, thought Violet, jumping bravely down beside William.

"Is everyone all right?" William shouted through the dog's barking. "No limbs broken?"

"I'm all right," Hettie said, pushing against a small rock. She sat up amid the mushrooms and peered over a speckled red top. "Arthur? Are you there?"

Papa waved slowly from his position by a large boulder. "I'm fine, Hettie. Don't worry. Now that we're here, let's do what we came for." They could only hear his words in the spaces when the dog paused for a breath.

Hettie sighed. What had they come for? That wild,

bouncing ride on the dog seemed to have turned her thoughts upside down. Violet, dog, Emily, Walter.

"Walter!" she shouted. "He could be near us right now!"

William said, "Let's think together, the way we did before."

Suddenly the dog's noise stopped at the same time as the chirring sound disappeared overhead. Something clambered through the upper limbs of the trees. Now that it was calmer, Papa called out, "On the count of three, call to Walter, asking him if he is near."

"All right, all right, I'm ready," said Violet impatiently.

Hettie straightened her shoulders, as Papa steadied himself with one hand. "One," he counted, "two, three!"

Walter, are you near? We are here, in the woods.

They sent their thoughts along the paths of moonbeams. Their words scattered down into Walter's hole, knocking against his head. But this time Walter was not asleep. He was fully, sadly, uncomfortably awake, waiting for something to happen. Things had crawled over him all day. Dampness from the trees had dripped onto his head. Some noisy bird had dropped a beetle husk onto his left arm. Later came the frightening sound of an animal; he wasn't sure what. It went, "Wruff, wruff, wruff!" and was accompanied by a fierce scratching nearby.

Walter, are you near? We are here, in the woods. The words spun into the tunnel.

He raised his head a fraction of an inch. His eyes shone and joy burst out of his mouth. *I am near that noisy animal. Come find me!* He tried to send a picture of his dark tunnel to his family.

"I think he's quite close, dear ones," exclaimed Papa. "I get a picture of something like a tunnel—dark and round."

"Yes, yes!" cried William, and he began to drag himself closer to the tree, inch by inch, calling out, "Walter? Walter? We're here."

Violet did not talk but pulled and pushed her way toward the dog.

Stiffly, Papa crawled over sticks and pebbles to the large tree where Hannah now sat, apparently waiting. Hettie pushed against a mushroom to move sideways, and it toppled to the ground. "Don't know my own strength!" she muttered, using her hands like paddles to push against the ground. Soon all four were under the tall pine.

"Do you see anything, William?" asked Papa. "I think your eyes are the sharpest. They are certainly the youngest."

William peered through the shadows on the forest floor. It all looked the same to him: blotches of darkness intermingled with the green of a low vine. The wind blew, making shadows move, and moonlight speckled the leaves and rocks.

Suddenly Violet cried out, "There, there!" pointing at a darker place to the left of the tree. "Could that be it?"

Papa peered at the spot. "Let's try!" They dragged themselves over and looked down. The shadow went into the earth, and in the moonlight they could see something lighter inside the tunnel.

Words caught in Hettie's throat. She was afraid to speak. What if it was a dead creature? What if it wasn't Walter?

William's mouth did not work. He tried to speak but couldn't. Only Papa seemed able to talk. In a soft croak he called out, "Walter? Is that you?"

The lighter shape within the darkness moved, and moonlight shone on two eyes.

"Papa! At last!" The words were jerky and rusty, like water that has been stopped up inside an old pipe and suddenly bursts out.

"Papa! Mama? William? Violet?"

Papa put a hand inside the tunnel and felt the round shape of a head. "Oh, my dear boy, it is you!"

Hettie began to sob and reached down to touch her son. A fragment of song floated up from his mouth. Violet peered inside and sang a lullaby from long ago.

Sticking his arm into the hole, William felt a hand. He shrieked, "Mama! There's a hand—all by itself."

"What? What?" called Mama.

"My hand fell off," said Walter calmly. "Mama will fix it. Papa will know what to do. Won't you?"

"Of course, son, of course," Papa replied. Then he said, "We've got to get him out and take him home. If we all pull together, I think we can lift him up. Now!"

They all grabbed Walter's shoulders, or whatever they could reach of him, and pulled hard. Slowly, bit by bit, he inched out of the hole. William wished he could close his eyes. First came Walter's head, wobbling on its stem. His eyes looked blurred. Then came his body, naked, the dun color of dust and ancient dirt. In a final rush, all of Walter was on the forest floor, all except his hand.

"Oh, Walter, my poor child!" Hettie sobbed. She clasped him to her, and his head knocked against her chest.

"Mama," he cried, "Mama!"

Papa coughed. "Someone's going to have to collect Walter's hand...from the tunnel." He made no move toward the round patch of shadow.

Violet turned her head away. It was one thing to survive a night in a tree; another to retrieve a piece of a... a skeleton! she thought.

Finally William sighed. "I must do it, then." If ever I am to deserve my heart, he thought. Reaching in, shuddering when he touched the thumb, William scraped the unattached hand up against the tunnel wall and out onto the forest floor.

"There," said Walter. "There it is. I've missed you, hand."

As they talked and embraced, they heard far away the faint sound of paws padding away into the forest.

chapter 19

WHEN EMILY went down the hall the next morning, she stopped and looked in the dollhouse. She remembered putting Papa and William on the chairs, with Hettie and Violet on the sofa. Now the chairs were empty. The sofa was bare.

Emily sat down by the dollhouse, and Hannah lay beside her. Were the dolls in the attic? Peering inside, Emily shifted blankets and moved beds around. No one was there. Shivers ran up and down Emily's back.

"Dolls?" Emily quavered. "Where are you?"

How could they leave on their own? As far as she

knew, the dolls could not move, much less walk. Maybe Rose took them. But why would she do that, now that she knew about dolls having feelings and wishing for things? Shaking her head, Emily stood and went downstairs to breakfast. Rose was already sitting at the table, eating granola.

She had to get Rose to herself, to talk. Even though it looked cool and misty outside, she asked, "Can we take our cereal out on the porch, Gran?"

"I don't see why not," Gran answered. "Help yourself, Emily."

She filled a blue bowl with granola and dribbled milk over the top. The most important thing about Gran's homemade cereal was to not douse it in too much milk so it stayed crunchy. "Come on, Rose." Emily pushed open the screen door and sat in a wicker chair.

"What's up?" Rose sat beside her. "Something's happened?"

"You didn't take the dolls out for a walk this morning, did you?"

Rose flushed. "Emily, I haven't *touched* them."

"There's not *one* doll left in the dollhouse, Rose, not one!" Emily ate a spoonful of granola.

"What?" Rose turned to look at her. "Where could they be?" After a moment's thought she added, *"How* could they be anywhere else? I don't think they can move, Emily."

"I don't understand it, either." Her sister frowned.

They sat in their chairs, looking over the gray field. Shreds of mist caught on the spiky stems of Queen

Anne's lace. Swallows dipped in and out of the fog, chittering.

"I guess we'd better go looking for them," Rose said dismally. "Though they could be *anywhere*."

"I'm glad I've got you, Rose." Emily put her hand on Rose's knee, and her sister patted it firmly. "I'd hate to do this all on my own."

"Me too," Rose said, giving Emily another comforting pat. "Let's get the dog and go looking. I guess I've eaten enough cereal to last me awhile."

Dumping their bowls in the dishwasher, the two girls set off down the steps. Hannah zigzagged ahead of them, nose to the ground.

"I wonder if the dolls are out looking for Walter." Rose said, brushing against a Queen Anne's lace.

"Maybe, but how? They can't walk."

"But they could ride!" Rose suddenly stopped. "On Hannah. Look at her fur! I bet the dolls gave her that fish William caught. They've gotten her to do things for them—I'm sure of it!"

"Rose, you are brilliant, just brilliant. Then where do we look?"

"Let Hannah show us. We'll follow her, and maybe she'll take us to the dolls." Rose ran after the dog.

"Hey, girls! Stop right there!" It was Mr. White, their next-door neighbor. At the head of the mowed path that went through Gran's meadow to the woods, he stood and waved his arms at them. "Take Hannah and go back to the house. We're burning off the brush in your grandmother's fields. This is no place for you girls to be."

"But, but...," Emily began. "We have to go to the woods!"

Dad looked up from the fire he was lighting near the stone wall. "Go back to the house, girls. Whatever you have to do can wait." He stepped back as the fire caught and began to spread across the field.

Rose looked at Emily. "I guess we'll have to try again later." She turned toward the house.

"But what about the dolls? If they're out in the woods and the fire..." Emily didn't finish, clapping her hand to her mouth. She took a step forward, then stopped. Flames sped along the side of the field, licking at the tall, dead grasses. The thick brown heads of dock flamed into torches. The fire jumped from the tops of grasses to clumps of bushes. Soon the field was a blaze of red and yellow, black smoke hurling into the air with sparks shooting through it. Dad and Mr. White stood well to one side, behind the fire.

"We'll have to wait, Emily. Come on." Rose tugged on her sister's jersey as Hannah jumped and whined at her side. "Come on. Let's go back to the house."

"What's that smell?" said Papa from his seat on the forest floor.

"What smell, dear?" Hettie said lazily, holding Walter close. He had lain in her lap all night long, his poor, faded head cradled in her arms. Hettie thought she had never known such happiness; something like molten gold seemed to flow through her body every time she felt

Walter in her lap. She was so happy, she did not worry about how they were going to get home again, now that the dog had gone and left them.

Papa stirred nervously. "How are we going to get home, and what is that smell?"

Violet wrinkled her nose. "It's like an iron left too long on a dress, Papa."

"The girls will find us," William said cheerfully. "They always do. We are in the same place we were when we first came looking with the girls and the dog yesterday. I expect they'll have the sense to come looking here again."

"Stop being so cheerful, William," Violet snapped. "Papa's right—there is a terrible odor in the air."

"A charred smell," added Papa.

" 'Charred'?" William said. "What does that mean, Papa?"

"He means something that has burned," Hettie explained, looking fondly at Walter's face. Even though his eyes had blurred and his mouth was faded, she could still see the features of her dear son. A little paint, some new clothes, someone to glue his hand back on, and he'd be as good as new. Arthur had said so.

"Burned!" Hettie caught herself and sat up straighter. "I don't like the sound of that, Arthur! *Burned* is a wicked, vicious word to people made out of wood!"

"I'm afraid so, dear heart," replied Papa in an agitated voice. "I think I even see smoke in the distance."

Violet let out a cry as the rest tried to look over their shoulders, with varying degrees of success. William was too stiff to turn around completely; Papa was already facing toward the field, but Hettie had her back to it. Walter was asleep on Mama's lap.

"It *is* smoke; it *is*!" Papa exclaimed. "And it's coming closer!"

With a great effort, William jerked himself around and stared beyond the edge of the woods. "It's red, Papa!" he shouted. "That means fire!"

The dolls stared at each other, horrified.

"Fire!" shouted Papa. "Fire, disaster, help, help!"

"There's no one to help us, Papa," Violet said. "We've got to do it ourselves."

"But what can we do?" Hettie's voice rattled in her throat, she was so afraid. "I don't want to burn!"

Walter stirred and said, "What's wrong, Mama?" He tried to curl back to sleep on his mother's lap, but she was moving too much and the frightened cries of the others kept waking him. "What's wrong?" he repeated.

"Fire, there's f-f-f-fire," Hettie sputtered.

William stared at the red flames racing toward them. He heard the crackling of dry grass and the explosive thunder of tinder going up in flames. His chest felt frozen and still. He must be brave, he must. Otherwise, how would he ever get his heart? He thought furiously, the thoughts dodging around inside his head like hard, bright things.

Hide, said one thought. Underground, said another. Get away from the heat and the fire.

"We must go back down the tunnel," William said, as

loudly as he could. "The only place we will be safe is in Walter's tunnel."

"Oh no, not there again!" wailed Walter. "I can't bear it! You just rescued me!"

But William was already lying on the floor of the forest, pulling himself forward with stiff hands. He inched toward the animal hole and dove headfirst, plummeting into the darkness. "Oh, oh!"

Violet managed to drag herself along, using the broken stems of seedlings. Once at the opening, she flung herself in.

Behind her Hettie wailed, "I can't, Arthur. I can't!" But Papa was beside her, pulling her along with his hands, now pushing, now shoving, somehow picking Walter up and thrusting him down the hole.

Behind him Papa could hear the crackle of flames and the confused shouts of men. Heat rushed at him on the wind, searing his cheeks and ears. He gave one last shove and pushed Hettie down the hole.

"Oh, oh!" she cried. As flames sped toward him, Papa pulled himself to the tunnel and inside. Darkness closed over him as he bumped against the bodies of the other dolls. He heard a high, wailing sound far away. And in the sky he saw drifts of black smoke, like dragon's breath.

chapter 20

THEY SAW that it was going wrong at the same time as the dolls. A gust of wind blew mist ahead of it and sent the flames racing to the edge of the meadow.

"Dad, Dad!" shouted Emily. "The fire's getting near the woods."

"I see!" Holding his shovel before him like a sword, Dad ran across the field, beating at the flames as he went. Mr. White took great leaping jumps across the smoldering grass to the line of fire. With his shovel he tried to bring the fire under control.

"Oh, I wish I could do something!" Emily said, and Rose took her hand.

"They'll get it out—don't worry, Emily. The dolls'll be all right." But Rose looked worriedly across the field at the two men who were bent over, hitting at flames.

Suddenly Dad called to the girls. "Call the fire department! This wind's too strong for us."

Turning, they raced for the house, banged through the kitchen door, and stopped in front of Mother. Rose cried, "Call the fire department! They need help! Quick, the dolls, Mother!"

Mother ran to the phone and dialed the fire department's number. Gran went to the door and looked out, with Emily and Rose beside her. Rose kept one hand firmly on the dog's collar.

"That's funny," Gran said. "There shouldn't be a strong wind on such a misty day. It's all right, girls; don't worry. They'll beat out some of the flames, and the fire department will be here soon."

Not long after, they heard the wailing of the fire truck coming up the road. It got louder and louder, then tires crunched on gravel as the truck swung up Gran's driveway. The truck skidded to a stop, and five men jumped out.

One calmly gave directions as two men snaked a long hose out of the truck's back. They ran with it down the path to the blazing meadow. Two others stayed by the pumper truck.

"Will they be all right?" Emily twisted the sleeve of Gran's blouse.

"Of course!" Gran said stoutly. "It's just a little grass fire. That won't hurt them."

"I don't mean Dad and Mr. White," Emily said. "I mean the dolls."

"The dolls? How can the fire possibly hurt them?" Gran asked.

"They're in the w-w-woods!" Rose sputtered. "If the fire gets there..." Her voice trailed off, and she looked at Emily.

But Emily was now on the top step, standing on tiptoe, staring out over the field. All of her will was directed toward the firefighters as they held out the long hose and sprayed a great jet of water over the blaze. Clouds of smoke roiled up to the sky, and Emily and Rose could hear the hiss of the dying fire. Back and forth the men sprayed water in a wide arc. As soon as one patch of the fire was quenched, they stepped rapidly over the smoldering earth and advanced on the next part of the fire.

"They're at the woods!" Rose stood on the step and grabbed Emily's shoulder. "Watch!" Hannah barked and whined, trying to squooge back inside the house.

They saw the men send a long stream of water over the trees at the edge of Gran's meadow. The trees were not on fire, yet, but the grass at the base of the trunks was blazing. Soon the flames had died, and the tree branches dripped water.

"There." Mother sighed behind them. "There. It's all out now, girls. No need to worry."

"But...," Rose began, then didn't finish. She could

not explain to her mother about the dolls being in the woods and how frightened they would be. Only Emily knew, and maybe Gran.

Two smoky, darkened figures stumbled out of the haze of smoke. Dad walked up to them, wiping his face. Mr. White followed, mopping his forehead with a sodden red bandana.

"I never saw anything go up so fast before," Mr. White said. "I am sorry, Mrs. Warren. It shouldn't have happened. I thought with the rain and this misty day that we'd be safe."

Emily ran to her father and hugged him tightly. His shirt had a sharp, strong smell, like danger.

"All right, hon, just a little fire." He grinned at his wife.

"You enjoyed it!" she accused him.

"No, no, not *too* much. I knew the firefighters would put it out," he said, letting go of Emily to take her arm.

"Come inside and get something cool." Gran led the way into the house. She sat the two men at the kitchen table and put out a tall pitcher of lemonade.

One of the firefighters poked his head inside the kitchen door. "Mrs. Warren? It's all out now. Everything's fine. You want to come look? Bill!" He shook his finger at Mr. White. "You know better than to burn in August—even on a wet day."

Mr. White blew his nose on his handkerchief. "I know better, Dan. I know better. But I thought we'd be OK. And we would've been except for that darn wind!"

Gran thanked the firefighters again, the men smiled and waved, and the door closed.

Hopping from one foot to another, Rose asked, "Can we go now, and see if . . . if the woods are safe now?"

Gran went to the door and looked at the smoldering meadow. "Bill? Henry? Can the girls go to the woods?"

"Not yet, Mrs. Warren." Mr. White shook his head.

"You girls'll have to wait a bit," said Dad. "Until the grass stops smoking. Bill says there could be hot spots left."

Emily stared at Rose, and her sister stared back. They could not rescue the dolls just yet.

"How long?" Emily asked, plunging her fingers into the thick fur on Hannah's back.

"Maybe by suppertime it will be cool enough," Dad said, and sipped his lemonade. "I'll have to check."

It wasn't until after they had eaten supper that Emily and Rose were allowed to go out to the woods, and only then after Dad had walked through the field, looking for hot spots.

"Go around the field, girls," he directed, "through that bunch of old apple trees. That will take you to the woods."

With Hannah at their side, they set off through the apple trees at the side of Gran's meadow. By making a long, curving path, they reached the edge of the woods.

"It's all different, Rose," said Emily sadly. "Look, the bittersweet's gone."

The old entrance to the woods, which used to be draped with thick bittersweet vines, was now charred. Behind the girls, the meadow spread out black and ruined.

"Come on!" Rose tugged on her sister's hand. "It's mostly the meadow that's burned. Maybe everyone is all right—wherever they are."

"Mmmm." Emily began to search from side to side.

Thrusting her nose into the leaves, the dog began to sniff busily. Occasionally she'd whuff and lift her head from the ground, blowing out bits of leaves and wood.

After a time Rose said dismally, "Em? How're we ever going to find them? They could be anywhere."

Emily stopped walking and asked, "Where would you go if you were a doll and saw a fire coming?"

"Where would I go? I don't even know if they can move, Emily!"

"But think. Under a rock?"

"Maybe," said Rose, and she ran up to the stone wall they'd sat on the other day. Lifting up different rocks, she peered beneath. "I don't see anything." Her voice bounced eerily off the wall.

"What's that?" called Papa from the darkness of the hole.

"What's what?" asked Violet in a crabbed voice.

"That noise. It sounds like our girls," Hettie answered.

"It is; it is!" William cried. "I'll think to them, to dear Rose!" Calling up all his strength, which he felt had ebbed out of the hole in that dreadful fire, he thought a picture of a tunnel beneath a tall tree. He called, *Rose, come find me, under the tree.*

In the midst of searching, Rose swiveled around in surprise. "Emily! They're here, somewhere near here. I heard him."

From the hole Hettie sent out her own call. *Bison, come rescue us, and I will feed you for the rest of your life.*

Hannah raised her head with a "whuff!" and trotted toward a near pine, with Rose following. Rose stopped by the trunk and waited while the dog snuffled the ground and began to dig.

Emily and Rose knelt beside her as the dog dug furiously in the fallen twigs and pine needles. Suddenly a tiny yellowed fragment flew through the air and landed in Rose's lap.

"Eeugh!" she cried. "What is it?"

Emily reached out and picked up the small shape. "I think—," she said, "I think it's a doll's hand."

Hannah stopped digging and sat back on her haunches, panting quietly. Emily leaned forward over a tunnel that the dog had uncovered.

"Look, Rose," she said in a strange voice.

Rose peered in. There, in the smudged darkness, were the upside-down dolls. Emily reached in.

"Here's Papa"—she laid him on Rose's lap—"and Hettie, Violet, and William." She settled them against Rose's stomach, patting them slightly. "All right now, everyone's OK. But where's Walter? He must be here. I don't want to do this; Rose, it's your turn."

Her sister looked at her, frowned, and gingerly put her hand inside the hole. "Eeugh!" she said again, taking out a faded, dirt-smeared doll. His eyes were blurred, his smile was crooked, but his arms were held out as Rose put him in her lap beside Hettie.

chapter 21

HOW DID they know?" Violet whispered that night, as they all lay in the living room. Rose and Emily had agreed that the dolls must sleep together their first night back in the dollhouse. So they had placed the mattresses side by side on the floor and put covers over the dolls.

"They just do," William said, sighing happily. "They know about dolls."

"Well," Violet reminded him, "Rose didn't *used* to know about us. Until you helped her."

Walter snuggled closer to Mama and Papa. "I forgot, Mama. About inside. I forgot about warm."

Hettie hugged him close. "Never again will you be cold. Never again will you be lost."

As Papa touched the back of Walter's head, he felt warm inside. "I told you," he said softly.

"Told us what?" Violet said.

"That I saw happiness like golden balloons over the dollhouse."

"But still," William began, his joy seeping away.

"William!" Violet exclaimed. "There are no *buts*. We are together again, and tomorrow morning I will hold Walter on my lap and sing him songs."

But I still don't have my heart, William thought to himself. How will I ever get one?

"What about Walter's hand?" William asked, a little sharply. Maybe *they* saw happiness like golden balloons over the dollhouse; *he* didn't—not yet.

"What about it?" Hettie murmured sleepily.

"Someone will have to glue it back on *and* fix his eyes *and* paint a new mouth on him."

"William!" chided Papa. "It doesn't do to remind people of what's missing. Make do with what you have."

"Well, he does need a mouth," William went on, "and eyes are always helpful."

Violet poked him in the back. "Let them be happy for one night!"

"All right, all right," William whispered. But he did not go to sleep. His head was full of hurtling thoughts. A heart for me. New eyes for Walter. Fire. Almost burned. My feet hurt. I was afraid.

In the morning—William knew it was morning by the slant of light across his body—the girls came and chattered excitedly outside the dollhouse. Then he was lifted into the air, wrapped in tissue paper, and placed gently in a shoe box.

"Mama, Papa!" he cried.

"Keep together, children. Remember to tell us where you are!" The voices wailed as the rest of the family was put into the same box. Then a cover closed over their heads, and they heard the girls talking.

"It's just till we get there, Emily. We can't let them bounce out."

Then came an older, thinner voice. "The dolls will be all right, girls. They've suffered worse these last days than being in a box with the cover tied down."

"But," came Emily's voice, "that's why I don't want them to suffer anymore. They've had enough, Gran!"

Violet nodded. Emily knew. Emily cared. Of all of them, she was the best. The dolls jostled inside the box, knocking against each other in spite of the tissue paper. Worst of all, to Violet, was the small unattached hand that clattered about, now touching her side, now hitting William.

The box bounced rhythmically, and there was a mechanical humming.

"What's that sound, Papa?" asked Violet.

"I'm not sure," he replied, but then William said excitedly, "It's a car, Papa. I remember I rode in one once in Alice's pocket."

The rest of the dolls sighed, comforted for a while. After a long time, noise and motion stopped. They were lifted up and jolted along. A door slammed, footsteps sounded against the floor, and a warm, hearty voice said, "Well, well, what have we here?" The top of the box was taken off and light shone in the dolls' faces.

"I see what you mean. Some smoke damage. This little one has seen more than that, hasn't he?"

Emily said, "He's spent many years in a fox's den or a woodchuck hole, we think."

"Mmmm, that would account for the stains on the porcelain—here, and here." He touched Walter. "And, of course, the paint on the eyes and mouth is quite damaged."

"You can fix it, can't you?" Emily asked anxiously.

Violet looked up at Emily, Rose, and a silver-haired man.

"Oh, I think so," said the man. "I've got to put a special solvent on the porcelain to remove the stains—lucky this one wasn't wood; he wouldn't have lasted if he were—and then repaint his features. All the rest could do with a nice bath."

"There, see, Violet?" Emily said cheerfully. "All you need is a nice bath to clean you up, and then you'll be as good as new."

Violet thought longingly of a new dress, maybe a red

one this time, with green trimmings and a bit of lace at the throat. The red would show how adventurous she was, how brave.

William thought longingly of his heart. If he wished hard enough, would this man give him one?

Papa thought longingly of his pipe that used to nestle so comfortingly in the pocket of his smoking jacket. He never smoked the pipe, of course, but it made him feel brave and elegant.

Hettie thought longingly of Walter. All she wanted was to have Walter back, with eyes that could see and a mouth that smiled—the way he used to be.

Walter did not wish for anything. He had what he wanted; he was home with his family again in a warm, dry place.

"All right," said the hearty voice. "Come back tomorrow, Rose and Emily, and this family will be ready by then."

"Good-bye, good-bye," chorused the girls. The door slammed, and the dolls were alone with the round-faced man with gold wire glasses and a bristling white mustache. He went to work right away.

"Mother doll, you come over here. All you need is a little cleaning to get the soot off your feet. The girls told me there was a brushfire. That must have been it. I imagine you were brave, like a mother lion." He sat Hettie on the edge of a dish, dipping her feet into a strong-smelling liquid. After she was clean, he dressed her in yellow silk.

Oh, thank you! I didn't feel brave, thought Hettie, *but*

I had to protect Walter after all he'd been through. I guess I can be brave if I have to.

While she sat there, the man put Papa nearby. He rubbed Papa's face, hands, and feet with a wet cloth, saying, "Tccch, tccch!" when he saw the black grime on his cloth. "You *have* had a time of it, Papa doll. What danger you've seen. I bet you were courageous, like a knight from long ago."

He took off Papa's blackened clothes and dressed him in long pants and a purple smoking jacket. He *tccch*ed to himself and asked, "Now where *did* I put that?" After rummaging about behind him, the doll maker turned and thrust a small, perfect pipe into Papa's jacket pocket.

You knew! Papa thought. *And you are right—I've seen danger just like King Arthur. Now I can live up to my name.*

Then the kind face smiled down at Violet. "Aren't you the pretty one? But I think there's more than just a pretty face here. I think you've faced some danger, too, hmmmm?"

I certainly have! And I never faltered, either. I have a heart as wide as the woods, thought Violet.

Carefully he took off her smoky clothes, cleaned her body with a strong-smelling cloth, and put her in a red dress.

Oh! thought Violet. *How did you know?*

He tucked a piece of lace around her neck and stitched it down tightly. "There, you needed something more daring than green. Something bright and cheerful, like your heart."

When he came to William, the man took him up and eyed him. He stripped off his clothes and *tut-tut*ted. "Why, what's missing here, young man? How did this happen?" He set him down on the counter, got some things from a shelf, and cleaned him all over, taking special care with his smoky feet. Dipping a brush in a jar of red paint, he drew a heart on William's chest. William shivered. He felt the brush make two bumps on top and two sloping lines down to a point at the bottom.

Oh, you knew, you knew JUST what I needed. Are you magic? thought William.

The man set him aside to dry and picked up Walter. "Well, you certainly are the challenge among this lot! How ever did you get into an animal's burrow? I guess you have a tale or two to tell." He laid Walter in a dish of strong-smelling liquid, letting him lie there for what seemed ages. While he was soaking, Walter heard the excited chatter of his family.

"Hettie, dear, did you see? I've got my pipe back and a smoking jacket, just like new!" exclaimed Papa.

"Walter, are you all right?" came Hettie's anxious voice.

Walter could not answer. Words seemed to have fled.

Violet chattered happily. "Can you all see my new red dress? 'Brave,' he called me 'brave'! "

And loudest of all came William's voice. "I've got a heart; I've got a heart, new and red with two bumps on top and a point at the bottom!"

The man dressed William in new sailor's pants and a

sailor's jacket to match. A small red kerchief fluttered at his neck.

"Look!" he crowed. "Maybe Rose'll take me sailing next time."

Then Walter was lifted up into the air, dried, and something hard and rough rubbed back and forth on his face and then his eyes. As the paper scratched, the outlines of the man's face blurred, disappeared, and Walter could see nothing.

"There, that will do nicely. Now, just a little paint." Walter heard the man's words and felt the tip of a wet brush on his face. The brush dipped down, then up, swooped over, and met at the first point. It made a circle in the middle, with a tiny dot inside. With that one eye Walter saw him clearly: the round, kind face; the gold glasses; the white mustache. The man leaned forward and painted another eye on the left side of his face.

"Now you'll see better, little one. And here's your mouth." This time, Walter saw him dip the fine brush in red paint and felt him draw a curving line just above his chin.

"There, always smile; never be sad," the man said. "I think you've had enough of sadness."

Searching through a box behind him, the man finally exclaimed, "Ah, here it is! A new hand for you, child." He glued it to the end of Walter's wrist and let it set. When at last Walter was dry, he was dressed in a green velvet suit and shiny black shoes.

Walter cried out, "Clothes, everyone. I haven't had clothes on in ages!"

With a weary sigh, the man pushed back his chair, took off his glasses, and rubbed his eyes thoroughly. "That's a job well done, if I say so myself. You're all ready and can go home tomorrow."

"Home!" sang the dolls. "At last!" And when the lights were turned out and the shop door locked, they continued to sing to each other about all the things they wanted to do when they got back to the dollhouse.

"Learn to draw," said William.

"Sing to Walter," said Violet.

"Make real muffins," said Hettie.

"Read about knights," said Papa.

"Be home," said Walter, "in my own bed with no beetles and no rain on my face."

chapter 22

"OH, THEY'RE PERFECT!" Emily exclaimed, picking up each doll in turn. "Thank you!" First she hugged the doll maker, then Rose, and then Gran.

"Thank you, Mr. Whittaker," Gran said. "Now we can take them home, girls."

Rose just stood there, staring at William. "Something's different about him. He seems...seems rounder somehow, or happier."

"Look." Mr. Whittaker gently opened William's new blue sailor jacket. Inside was the freshly painted red heart.

"Oh, *that's* what he needed!" cried Rose. "I knew it was something, but I wasn't sure what. I always thought he wanted to go fishing."

Gran eyed her curiously, said nothing, and paid the doll maker. Once settled in the car and heading home, Emily cradled the box containing the dolls. When they parked, Rose opened the car door for Emily.

"Thanks." Her sister stepped out carefully. "We don't want to shake up the dolls."

"See you later, girls," Gran said, smiling. "Remember to come down for lunch."

"All right." Rose ran up the stairs after her sister. She couldn't wait to get the dolls settled in their house.

Emily knelt by the open front and lifted the top of the box. First she took out Hettie and sat her in a living-room chair with a small book she'd made for her. Rose put William in the other chair, with a tiny pencil in his hand and a small tablet of paper.

"He wants to draw," she explained. "I just know it—don't ask me how."

"I don't need to ask you how; I know," replied Emily. Lifting Violet carefully, she arranged her on the purple sofa. The bright red of her dress stood out in the shadowy room.

"Doesn't Violet look like a princess?" asked Emily.

"Or a queen," said Violet. "I think I look like a queen. Papa, what do you think?"

Papa, who had been put beside Violet, was a little abashed at his daughter's finery. He coughed and said, "You do look rather like a queen."

"Don't get airs, Violet," said William from his chair. "We're just dolls, remember?"

"Hmmmph!" flounced Violet, unable to find a satisfactory reply. She wanted to smooth the lace at her throat but knew she must wait until the girls had gone.

"Here's Walter." Emily sat him on Mama's lap. He seemed to lean back against her new silk dress, letting his head sink into the hollow below her shoulder. Hettie sang softly to him.

"Oh, I want him on *my* lap!" cried Violet.

"Later, dear," soothed Hettie. "Now he needs to be with his mama."

"You can have him tomorrow, Violet," said Emily, remembering her dream about the dolls.

"There." Rose sat back on her heels and sighed.

"They look perfect," Emily said in a mournful tone.

"I know, all complete somehow," complained Rose.

They stared at each other, not sure why they didn't feel gloriously happy now that Walter was back and the dolls were safe. Hannah nudged them from behind and whined.

"She wants some attention, too." Rose thumped the dog on her back. "We can't give it all to the dolls, you know."

"I know," sighed Emily. "And now we've got to start thinking about school and what we're going to wear on the first day..." Her voice trailed off.

"It won't be so bad." Rose stood up and brushed down her dress. "We're brave. We found Walter, we solved the mystery, and the dolls didn't get burned up. We can do things, you know, Emily." Her words were brave, but at the back of her mind was a black cloud as she thought of the first day of school and the horror of walking past all those unknown people.

"But now there's no more mystery, Rose." Emily got to her feet. "I'd like to solve another mystery."

"Life is full of mystery and death," said William from his chair.

"A.M.," said Violet.

"*Amen,*" corrected William.

"A.M., *amen*—what difference does it make?" Violet grinned. "They're still going to play with us—maybe they'll take us on adventures. I rather liked going on those little trips."

"To the graveyard, dear?" Hettie protested.

"Well, maybe not the *graveyard,* but I liked sleeping outside in a nest of leaves in the tree. I saw the stars come out," Violet said dreamily.

"So did I," replied Hettie. "When we were traveling on the bison's back."

"*Traveling on the Bison's Back,*" said Papa. "Sounds like an account of going west, dear."

"Maybe it is." Hettie straightened. "I could write it down in this little book Emily gave me."

"Then she'll have to solve the mystery of how those words got there!" exclaimed William. "We are going to have fun."

"What is 'fun,' Mama?" Walter asked from his mother's lap.

"Things you like to do, dear, that make you smile.

Such as playing with a ball or listening to me sing." She began to croon a lullaby.

"We'll have fun," Rose announced, echoing William. "It won't be so bad. Maybe we could bring Hannah to school one day. Kids always like dogs, and it would give us something to talk about."

"Maybe. Will we make friends, Rose?"

"Of course we will! We always do." Then Rose looked at William. If she were afraid on the first day of school, she could always put him in her pocket. He could give her courage, if she needed it.

Then she started.

"What? What is it?" Emily touched her arm.

Rose did not answer. She wasn't sure, but she thought she had seen William wink one gleaming eye at her.